FINDING PEACE

FINDING SERIES #3

SLOANE KENNEDY

CONTENTS

Copyright   v
Finding Peace   vii
Trademark Acknowledgements   ix
Author's Note   xi
Series Reading Order   xiii
Series Crossover Chart   xvii

Chapter 1   I
Chapter 2   9
Chapter 3   26
Chapter 4   37
Chapter 5   53
Chapter 6   67
Chapter 7   84
Chapter 8   99
Chapter 9   113
Chapter 10   128
Chapter 11   138
Epilogue   150

Sneak Peek   153
Trigger Warning   155
Prologue   157

About the Author   163
Also by Sloane Kennedy   165

Published in the United States by Sloane Kennedy
All rights reserved. This book or any portion thereof may not be reproduced or used in any manner whatsoever without the express written permission of the publisher except for the use of brief quotations in a book review.

Cover Images: © curaphotography © Markomarcello

Cover Design: © Jay Aheer, Simply Defined Art

ISBN-13:
978-1541062351

ISBN-10:
1541062353

FINDING PEACE

Sloane Kennedy

TRADEMARK ACKNOWLEDGEMENTS

The author acknowledges the trademarked status and trademark owners of the following trademarks mentioned in this work of fiction:

Google
Mercedes

AUTHOR'S NOTE

Although I have done my best to research some of the medical issues discussed in this book, I am not a medical professional and any liberties taken with reference to medical conditions were done for the sake of the story.

SERIES READING ORDER

All of my series cross over with one another so I've provided a couple of recommended reading orders for you. If you want to start with the Protectors books, use the first list. If you want to follow the books according to timing, use the second list. Note that you can skip any of the books (including M/F) as each was written to be a standalone story.

Note that some books may not be readily available on all retail sites

Recommended Reading Order (Use this list if you want to start with "The Protectors" series)
1. Absolution (m/m/m) (The Protectors, #1)
2. Salvation (m/m) (The Protectors, #2)
3. Retribution (m/m) (The Protectors, #3)
4. Gabriel's Rule (m/f) (The Escort Series, #1)
5. Shane's Fall (m/f) (The Escort Series, #2)
6. Logan's Need (m/m) (The Escort Series, #3)
7. Finding Home (m/m/m) (Finding Series, #1)
8. Finding Trust (m/m) (Finding Series, #2)

9. Loving Vin (m/f) (Barretti Security Series, #1)
10. Redeeming Rafe (m/m) (Barretti Security Series, #2)
11. Saving Ren (m/m/m) (Barretti Security Series, #3)
12. Freeing Zane (m/m) (Barretti Security Series, #4)
13. Finding Peace (m/m) (Finding Series, #3)
14. Finding Forgiveness (m/m) (Finding Series, #4)
15. Forsaken (m/m) (The Protectors, #4)
16. Vengeance (m/m/m) (The Protectors, #5)
17. A Protectors Family Christmas (The Protectors, #5.5)
18. Atonement (m/m) (The Protectors, #6)
19. Revelation (m/m) (The Protectors, #7)
20. Redemption (m/m) (The Protectors, #8)
21. Finding Hope (m/m/m) (Finding Series, #5)22. Defiance (m/m) (The Protectors #9)

Recommended Reading Order (Use this list if you want to follow according to timing)
1. Gabriel's Rule (m/f) (The Escort Series, #1)
2. Shane's Fall (m/f) (The Escort Series, #2)
3. Logan's Need (m/m) (The Escort Series, #3)
4. Finding Home (m/m/m) (Finding Series, #1)
5. Finding Trust (m/m) (Finding Series, #2)
6. Loving Vin (m/f) (Barretti Security Series, #1)
7. Redeeming Rafe (m/m) (Barretti Security Series, #2)
8. Saving Ren (m/m/m) (Barretti Security Series, #3)
9. Freeing Zane (m/m) (Barretti Security Series, #4)
10. Finding Peace (m/m) (Finding Series, #3)
11. Finding Forgiveness (m/m) (Finding Series, #4)
12. Absolution (m/m/m) (The Protectors, #1)
13. Salvation (m/m) (The Protectors, #2)
14. Retribution (m/m) (The Protectors, #3)
15. Forsaken (m/m) (The Protectors, #4)
16. Vengeance (m/m/m) (The Protectors, #5)
17. A Protectors Family Christmas (The Protectors, #5.5)

18. Atonement (m/m) (The Protectors, #6)
19. Revelation (m/m) (The Protectors, #7)
20. Redemption (m/m) (The Protectors, #8)
21. Finding Hope (m/m/m) (Finding Series, #5)
22. Defiance (m/m) (The Protectors #9)

SERIES CROSSOVER CHART

Protectors/Barrettis/Finding Crossover Chart

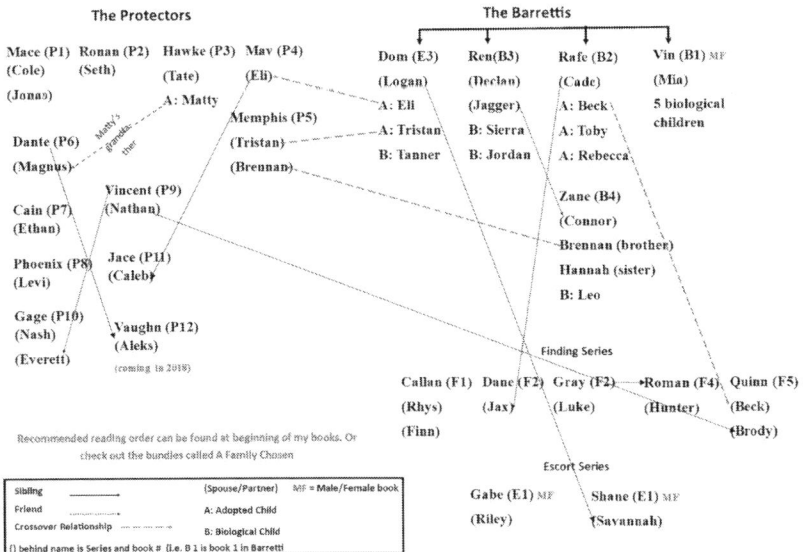

The Protectors

The Barrettis

Mace (P1)   Ronan (P2)   Hawke (P3)   Mav (P4)

(Cole)   (Seth)   (Tate)   (Eli)

(Jonas)

A: Matty

Dante (P6)

(Magnus)

Memphis (P5)

(Tristan)

(Brennan)

Vincent (P9)

(Nathan)

Cain (P7)

(Ethan)

Jace (P11)

(Caleb)

Phoenix (P8)

(Levi)

Gage (P10)

(Nash)

Vaughn (P12)

(Aleks)

(Everett)

(coming in 2018)

Matty's grand-father

Dom (E3)   **Ren(B3)**   **Rafe (B2)**   **Vin (B1)** MF

(Logan)   (Declan)   (Cade)   (Mia)

A: Eli   (Jagger)   A: Beck   5 biological

A: Tristan   B: Sierra   A: Toby   children

B: Tanner   B: Jordan   A: Rebecca

Zane (B4)

(Connor)

Brennan (brother)

Hannah (sister)

B: Leo

Finding Series

Callan (F1)   Dane (F2)   Gray (F2)   Roman (F4)   Quinn (F5)

(Rhys)   (Jax)   (Luke)   (Hunter)   (Beck)

(Finn)   (Brody)

Recommended reading order can be found at beginning of my books. Or check out the bundles called A Family Chosen

Escort Series

Gabe (E1) MF   Shane (E1) MF

(Riley)   (Savannah)

Sibling	————	(Spouse/Partner)	MF = Male/Female book
Friend	·············	A: Adopted Child	
Crossover Relationship	··· ··· ··· ···	B: Biological Child	
() behind name is Series and book # (i.e. B 1 is book 1 in Barretti			

CHAPTER 1

"*S*on of a bitch!"

Gray Hawthorne let off another string of curses as he felt the seatbelt slam against his chest, his foot jamming the brake pedal down as far as it could go. Although his gut was telling him not to jerk the wheel to the right, he did so anyway and his only indication that he hadn't run over the big dog standing in the middle of the road was the fact that he didn't feel his pickup truck's wheels plowing over the dog's body. And since the dog didn't let out a scream of pain, he was hopeful he'd jolted out of his maudlin thoughts quickly enough to avoid causing the animal any kind of injury at all. His truck skidded to a stop on the gravel shoulder and he managed to twist the wheel enough to keep the vehicle from rolling into the ditch.

"Jesus Christ," he muttered as he put the truck in park and tried to catch his breath. His whole body shook from the adrenaline rush of the near miss but he managed to lift his eyes to the rearview mirror. Damn dog was still standing in the exact same spot in the middle of the road. Although there wasn't a lot of traffic on the back country road leading to his cabin, Gray knew that the dog would have a very short lifespan if it didn't get its ass off the blacktop. Between the ranchers and the hunters that lived in and visited the area, a dog's life was on the very low end of the value scale.

Gray managed to release the seatbelt that was still strangling him, though it took several tries. He checked for traffic and then got out of the truck. The dog was less than a hundred yards away barking incessantly.

"Come here, girl," Gray called as he squatted. He didn't know much about dogs, but he figured making himself seem as unintimidating as possible was the way to go. But it didn't matter because even though the dog turned its big head his way, it didn't budge and it never stopped barking. Between the close call and the anxiety that had been rolling through him long before he'd lain eyes on the animal, Gray felt an urge just to get in his truck and keep going. It wasn't the good guy thing to do but that was a label he'd given up a long time ago when he'd learned that good guys didn't win in his world. They didn't even get to play the fucking game.

Gray rose and reached for the door handle before he let out another foul curse. He sucked in a breath and then began moving towards the dog, his eyes scanning the road both in front and behind him for cars.

"Come here, sweetie," he called but the dog continued to ignore him. As he got closer, he could see it was a German Shepherd and that it was enormous. But it was also a mess. Mud caked its fur and even with its thick coat, Gray could see its ribs protruding. Gray tried lowering himself again but the dog didn't budge. It did stop barking however, and Gray couldn't decide if that was a good or bad thing. The dog's golden brown eyes shifted between him and the grove of trees just off to the side of the road. It was the same thing the animal had been looking at when his truck came flying over the slight rise in the road.

"Good girl," Gray whispered once he was within a couple feet. To his surprise, the dog trotted up to him and sat down at his feet. But instead of barking, it began whining and when it pressed against his hand with its cold muzzle, Gray ran his fingers over the animal's head.

The second he removed his fingers, the dog barked and then took several steps towards the side of the road.

"Okay, Lassie, I get you," Gray drawled. He followed the dog and wasn't surprised when it disappeared down into the ditch. He was half expecting to find another dog, maybe an injured one, lying in the heavy brush that was so predominant in this area. But he knew as soon as he reached the side of the road and looked down that the curled up form lying among the foliage wasn't a dog at all.

~

*L*uke Monroe felt cold all over even though it was unbearably hot outside. Except his face – it just felt wet...again. Damn dog. If the mangy mutt wasn't licking his face, then it was going after any exposed skin it could find. He tried to roll away from the dog's sticky tongue but pain seared across his side and he bit back a moan. He could feel sharp rocks digging into his body but couldn't process where they'd come from. The last thing he remembered was walking along the side of the road, the hot pavement reflecting the heat back up at him so it felt like he was trudging through a furnace. There'd been a slight breeze but it had only made the dry heat that much more sweltering and he'd cursed himself for not having the sense to search out a couple more water bottles besides the two he'd stashed in his duffle bag.

Of course, two should have been plenty considering his final destination hadn't been more than half a day's walk away. As he had gotten closer to his destination, he'd actually felt little zings of excitement go through his body at the prospect of a soft bed and a hot meal tonight instead of another night trying to fall asleep on the cold ground with the contents of his last MRE sitting like lead in his belly. But truth be told, he'd been even more enthralled with the idea of finally feeling safe, of finally not having to be looking over his shoulder all the time. To have the one man he trusted above all others watching his back like he had when they were kids.

3

He still wasn't sure why he was surprised to find that his last hope for salvation had turned out to be wishful thinking. Luke had known it the instant he saw the police car pulling onto the dirt road that led up to the CB Bar Ranch and recognized the familiar face behind the wheel – the one that hadn't changed much in the seven years since he'd last seen it. At least he'd been smart enough to take cover in a line of trees on the other side of the road while he'd scouted out the area. Once the car had been out of sight, he'd started the long walk back towards town while his weary brain tried to come up with plan B which probably should have been his plan A, since all he'd managed to do in the last three days was spend what little money he had left on the bus ticket that had only gotten him to Billings. After that, he'd hitchhiked with a variety of truckers who'd either wanted to talk his ear off or propositioned him. He'd lucked out with the last trucker though, because the old man had simply dropped him off with a few words wishing him well before he'd continued on his journey west, while Luke had gone south on the highway that would lead him to the small town of Dare, Montana.

Luke hadn't actually seen much of the town since he'd hadn't wanted to risk being noticed so he'd stayed on the outskirts and had only gone into a gas station to fill up his water bottles and get cleaned up. It had taken several hours to head out of town towards his destination but since that had turned out to be a bust, he'd been left with no choice but to retrace his steps back to Dare so that he could spend his last few dollars on a much needed meal. But between the gnawing hunger and lack of water, his body had clearly had other thoughts and for the life of him, he couldn't remember anything after seeing black spots dancing across his eyes. Now he just needed to figure out if rolling down the embankment had caused even more damage to his already battered body.

"Hey-"

Luke heard the voice only a fraction of a second before he felt fingers close over his upper arm. He heard a grunt as he lashed out with his right hand and shoved his attacker away from him while he scrambled to his feet. Ignoring the agony that shot through his side at the move, he scrambled to his feet and reached for the gun tucked in the waistband of his jeans. A wave of dizziness swept through him as he aimed his Beretta at the man who was still bent over on the ground, his hand pressed against his chest.

∼

*G*ray tried to suck in a breath but the pain was too overwhelming and he could only helplessly gasp as he willed himself not to panic. The fucker packed one hell of a punch and Gray had no doubt he'd end up with a bruise where the guy's fist had connected with the right side of his chest. But the need for oxygen became an afterthought when he looked up and saw the gun aimed at his head. Gray forced himself to drop his hand and he held both arms out, palms open. Standing wasn't an option yet since pain continued to radiate through his body but he was surprised when the man instantly lowered the gun and held it loosely by his leg.

"Who are you?" the guy snapped as he scanned the area around them. Probably looking to see if Gray was alone or not.

Gray slowly lowered one hand back to his chest as he tried to stand but couldn't manage it. He was shocked when the guy stepped forward and wrapped an arm around him and eased him up from the crouching position he'd been stuck in.

"Try not to take deep breaths," the man said as he used his hand to push up the T-shirt Gray was wearing. Under any other circumstances, the rough fingertips dragging over his skin and the husky voice near his ear would have turned Gray on but all he felt was fear as the immediate threat of being shot dissipated and his air-starved lungs refused to heed his order to suck in some much needed oxygen.

"Look at me," the guy suddenly said as he moved so he was standing in front of Gray. "Slow, short breaths like this," he said as he demonstrated. Gray didn't miss the fact that the man was still brandishing the gun but his gray-blue eyes never left Gray's so Gray focused on them instead and tried to mirror his breathing to match the other man's. To his relief, air began moving more freely through

5

his chest. The man seemed satisfied and dropped his eyes to skim over the place on Gray's side where his fingers were still gently probing.

"Does your whole chest hurt or just here?" the man asked as his warm hand settled over the spot just beneath Gray's pectoral muscle.

"Just there," Gray managed to get out. The pain was still intense but it was indeed localized to where the guy had hit him and although it still hurt to breathe, at least he could actually manage it now.

"I don't think your ribs are broken but they could be cracked or bruised. You'll need a chest X-ray to know for sure."

Gray shoved the guy's hand away. "I'm fine," he snapped even though he knew it wasn't the smartest attitude to have since the guy had yet to put the gun away. But he was also royally pissed. "You go around pulling guns on everyone who tries to help you?" he managed to wheeze between choppy breaths.

The man stepped back and then looked down at the gun in his hand as if just realizing it was there. He tucked it behind his back and said, "You shouldn't have touched me."

Ungrateful bastard.

"And I didn't need help," he added.

Gray snorted and shook his head. "So you just like taking naps in ditches?" he bit out. When the guy didn't respond, Gray said, "You know what, fuck it. Keep your dog off the road."

"She's not my dog."

Gray nearly laughed at that but his ribs still hurt too badly so he just glanced down at the German Shepherd that was practically pressed up against the guy's leg. "Right," Gray murmured as he turned to go. But as he began to climb the slight incline, a wave of heat passed over him and his stomach rolled violently. His vision dimmed as he took his next step and he closed his eyes desperately to try to maintain his equilibrium. It was no use though and he tried to put his hands out in an effort to break his fall as his knees buckled. But his body never made contact with the ground as an arm wrapped around him from behind and kept him upright. He knew he should either say thank you or shove the guy away but all he could do was turn his head to the side as he leaned over and threw up.

6

~

*L*uke managed to maintain his hold on the other man as he continued to retch long after the contents of his stomach had been emptied. Although the man was sweating profusely, his skin felt cold and clammy. Luke had hit the guy pretty hard but he was almost certain he hadn't caused any injury to any internal organs...almost.

After several minutes, the man's spasms began to ease and Luke felt his own side burn with pain as the man pressed back against him, his full weight sinking onto the arm Luke still had wrapped around his waist.

"I'm okay," the guy said as he tried to pull away but as soon as Luke loosened his hold, he became wobbly again.

"I need to get you to the hospital," Luke said as he glanced around the ground to search out his duffle bag.

"No," the man said quickly. A strange sensation passed through Luke as he felt the man's fingers resting on his forearm but he ignored it.

"I could have caused some kind of internal injury-"

"No. I was feeling sick before...it must be the stomach flu. I'm okay."

Luke wasn't convinced but when the guy pushed his arm away, he released him. The stranger teetered back and forth a bit but then steadied. Luke kept his eye on him, quickly taking a couple of steps back and snagging his bag off the ground. As the man began walking back up the incline, Luke could see he was struggling and he wrapped his arm around him once more.

"I'm fine," was the weak protest, the words barely a whisper, the stranger's skin deathly pale. They'd barely made it up to the top of the ditch when he began throwing up again but since there was nothing left in his stomach, all he could do was dry heave.

Luke spied a pick-up truck sitting farther up the road and got the man moving in that direction as soon as the episode passed. By the time they made it to the vehicle, the man was breathing heavily and

Luke didn't miss the grunts of pain. Guilt went through him at the knowledge that the vomiting was likely making his injury hurt all the more. Luke could feel wetness seeping through his own shirt but he ignored it, taking nearly all the man's weight on himself as he reached for the passenger side door. It was a struggle but he managed to get him into the seat.

"You're bleeding," the stranger said softly as his glazed eyes fell to Luke's side. Luke glanced down and saw that a small amount of blood had seeped through his shirt. He'd definitely torn his stitches but when he pulled his shirt up, he sighed in relief to see that most of them were still intact. Looking up, he saw that the man's gaze was on the injury and when Luke dropped the shirt to cover it, the man's hazel eyes lifted to his. But anything he was about to say died on his lips as he began retching once more.

CHAPTER 2

*G*ray felt his stomach roll as he swung his legs over the side of the bed but blessedly, he didn't feel the tell-tale sign of bile creeping up the back of his throat so he didn't make a dash for the bathroom. Instead, he closed his eyes and tried to swallow away the dryness in his mouth along with the distinct metallic flavor that seemed to permeate his taste buds. It was just more proof that everything the doctors had been telling him was true and he bit back the disappointment that he hadn't been able to prove them wrong. His entire life had been about telling the people who said he couldn't do something – that he'd never be anything – to fuck off. But this…well, this he could tell to fuck off but it wouldn't matter if he whispered it or shouted it at the top of his lungs. His disease would always come out on top.

As he let his eyes adjust to the darkness, Gray listened for any sounds that would indicate his unexpected guest was still around. It had been humiliating enough to throw up in front of the guy even the one time. But to have kept on doing it in the truck – his truck that he'd had no choice but to let the stranger drive – was the icing on the cake. Or so he'd thought at the time. Then they'd gotten back to his place and instead of heeding the guy's warning to wait for him to help him out of the truck, Gray had shoved the door open in a pathetic act of defiance and hadn't even made it a step before a wave of dizziness swept through him and he'd fallen to his knees on the parched earth that was his driveway. Heavy black combat boots had appeared in his line of vision but fortunately there was nothing left in his stomach to expel, so at least the guy's shoes didn't track puke all through the cabin when he'd helped Gray to the bathroom.

At that point, Gray hadn't given a shit about pride anymore and after he'd hung over the toilet for several long, agonizing minutes, he'd curled himself into a ball on the wonderfully cool, tile floor and closed his eyes and prayed it was over. It wasn't of course – not after an hour, not even after two. And then he'd simply lost track of time as well as the will to care. He hadn't cared about the rough hands that had held him upright as he heaved next to nothing into the porcelain bowl and he hadn't cared about the cool washcloth pressed to his forehead. The only time he'd even tried to speak was when the guy had placed a glass of water against his lips and told him to drink. As good as the water had felt against his tongue for the split second before it tasted like someone had shoved a handful of coins in his mouth, he hadn't seen the point since it stayed in his stomach only for a few minutes each time. But his brief protest hadn't even seemed to register with the stranger because he kept forcing Gray to drink and then wrapped an arm around Gray's chest so his body was protected from the edge of the toilet seat. Everything after that was a blank. He wasn't even sure how he'd managed to get to his bed but he had a sneaking suspicion.

Gray forced himself to his feet but kept a hand on the nightstand as his lax muscles tried to recover. His head started to spin but luckily the nausea didn't worsen and within a few minutes, the lightheaded-ness passed and he managed to take a few steps forward without fall-ing. His bedroom door was slightly ajar which definitely wouldn't have been the way he left it because he always shut himself into a room even after years of living alone.

By the time he reached the door, he was ready to turn back around and crawl into bed again but the curiosity to see if he still had any personal possessions left was too great. While a lot of his smaller valuables were tucked away in boxes, he'd been out of it for so long that the mystery man could have taken his time cleaning him out. He just really hoped the man had left his books behind. Laptop, big screen TV, tablet – losing that shit would suck but if the guy had taken his books…

The cabin wasn't huge in any sense of the word but it wasn't until Gray reached the kitchen that he heard the sound and it took him several long seconds to figure out what it was. He glanced out the window and was relieved to see his truck sitting in the driveway but the tell-tale sound of metal biting through wood had his gut churning with anxiety. A glance at the clock on the stove showed it was only one o'clock in the afternoon. He couldn't be a hundred percent sure since he didn't know what day it was but in all likelihood, it had only been twenty-four hours since he'd been staring down the barrel of a gun. The gun whose owner apparently hadn't left yet.

Gray glanced around the kitchen for his phone. He'd left it sitting in the cup holder in his truck when he'd gotten out to check on the dog so he had no idea if it had made it inside or not. There was a landline in the cabin but he hadn't even considered getting it activated since he always had his cell phone which had ended up having decent reception even in the mountainous region. His only other option to seek help was if he could get to his laptop which he'd left sitting on the coffee table in the living room. But even as he began moving, it registered that if the guy had wanted to do anything to him, he sure as hell had had plenty of opportunities. And so far everything in his bedroom and the kitchen had looked untouched and completely normal.

It took only half a dozen steps to reach the living room but it definitely wasn't untouched. Most everything was still as he'd left it. Laptop on the table, flat screen still attached to the wall, his three boxes of books stacked neatly near the desk against the far window. But it was the pile of tree branches on the floor between the TV and the desk that had his attention. He estimated them to be about five feet long and all of them had a clean, straight cut on one end.

"Oh, hey."

Gray whirled around at the husky voice behind him and had to reach out to grab onto his desk to keep from falling. He hadn't even heard the door open because he'd been too busy trying to figure out what the hell a bunch of trees were doing in his house.

"You look better," the guy said as he moved past Gray and leaned the branch he'd been holding in one hand against the wall. In his other hand was a flatter piece of wood. And tucked in the waistband of his pants was the gun.

Gray was at a loss for words as he watched the man lean down and start picking up the other branches so he could lean them against the wall. A wet nose pressed into Gray's hand and he glanced down to see the German Shepherd sniffing him. He let his hand skim over the dog's head.

"You okay with her being in here?" the guy asked and Gray snapped his eyes up to see the man studying him.

Was he okay with the dog being in here? Shit, he wasn't okay with anything that was going on.

"I was able to get her cleaned up a bit," the man offered and Gray looked down again and saw that the dog did indeed look better than it had.

"Did you use my shampoo on her?" Gray asked in surprise as he recognized the woodsy scent wafting off the animal.

"Yeah. Found it in your shower. Worked better than I thought it would."

"It should," Gray muttered. "It's a hundred bucks a bottle."

The guy actually snorted but didn't respond. Instead he said, "You should drink something. You're bound to be dehydrated."

The reminder of the situation had Gray drawing up as straight as he could considering that even just the thought of trying to drink anything had his nausea coming back in full force.

"You mind if I take a look?" the guy suddenly asked and then he was standing only a few inches away from Gray. The sudden punch of desire that slammed through Gray was unexpected. It wasn't that the man wasn't his type since Gray wasn't at all discriminating – a nice dick, tight ass and fuckable mouth had always been his only require-ments. But that was before...and this guy had all that in spades and more. He was big – at least 6'2 and his wide shoulders and chest led down to a trim waist. The dark green T-shirt he was wearing was snug and hinted at generous, well-defined muscles.

The man's face wasn't handsome in the classical sense but his wide, stubble-covered jaw had Gray wanting to know how it would feel brushing over his skin as those full lips explored him. Stormy grayish-blue eyes were surrounded by black lashes that looked too long to belong to a man, but somehow seemed to work for this guy. Dark brows just a shade lighter than his closely cropped hair were arched in perfect unison over his hooded gaze which was studying Gray with curiosity. It took Gray a long moment to realize the guy had asked him a question.

"What?"

"Can I take a look at your ribs?"

The man's hand was already reaching for Gray's shirt and it wasn't until then that Gray realized he hadn't even thought to put on clothes when he'd gotten out of bed. At least he was wearing sweats and a T-shirt but he sure as hell hadn't been wearing them yesterday when he'd been hunched over the toilet. He was about to ask the guy if he'd somehow managed to miraculously undress and redress himself when warm fingers pressed against the side of his chest.

"Fuck," Gray said as he pulled back.

"Still hurt?"

"Yeah," Gray mumbled as he tried to ignore the tingling where the guy's fingers had been. At least he didn't have to worry about trying to hide a hard-on around the guy. A fucked up silver lining he supposed. "Not as bad as yesterday, though," he added when he saw the look of guilt in the man's gaze. He had no idea why he cared either way.

"You should still get them checked out."

The fingers kept probing Gray's side. "Are you a doctor or some-thing?" he asked when it occurred to him that the way the guy was touching him was very specific – like he was looking for something.

The man shook his head. "Just had some field training."

"Military?"

A brief nod. The admission should have made Gray feel better but then he noticed the jagged scar that started at the man's temple and disappeared into his hair. A memory from yesterday hit him – the guy had been bleeding when he'd helped Gray into the truck.

"Are you able to take a deep breath?"

Gray was jolted from his thoughts when he felt the man's warm breath skim over his flesh as he continued to examine the bruised flesh. Shit, shit, shit – he could not be attracted to this man.

Pushing down his T-shirt, Gray took several steps back. "It's fine," he said firmly.

Hard eyes pinned his for a moment but he couldn't tell what the other man was thinking. Another tremor of fear went through him and he reflexively took another step back. Something suddenly flashed through the man's gaze before his expression went blank again and Gray couldn't quite be sure what he'd seen. Disappointment? That couldn't be right.

The man turned back to the branches he'd leaned against the wall and started collecting them one by one until they were all piled in his arms. "I wasn't sure where you wanted your car keys so I stuck them in your desk drawer," he said as he jutted his chin towards Gray's desk and then turned to head for the door. "Your phone is in there too," he added.

Before he could react, the guy was striding through the wide open front door. Gray watched him go and then pulled open the drawer and saw that his phone and keys were there. Indecision went through him and then he hurried after the guy. He stepped outside and heard the sound of wood hitting more wood next to the cabin. By the time he made his way down the porch steps, the man was back and brushing past him, his bag slung over his shoulder, the dog at his side. It took every bit of strength Gray had left to catch up to him and step in his path. He was glad when the man stopped instead of moving around him or shoving him out of the way.

"What was the wood for?"

The guy eyed him for a long moment and then said, "Bookshelf."

14

"A bookshelf?" Gray asked in astonishment.

"You've got a lot of boxes marked books but I didn't see any place for you to put them. I found a couple of fallen white birch trees on your property that were still in pretty good shape so…"

The man's voice dropped off and Gray was surprised when he lowered his eyes. "Figured it might tide you over till yours came or you bought one." He shook his head and moved around Gray again. "I left the wood out by the woodpile in back – you can just toss it in your fireplace so it doesn't go to waste."

For the first time in his life, Gray was truly and utterly speechless. And he felt like a complete shit. Without turning he called, "What's your name?"

When there was no answer, he did turn but was surprised that the guy had actually stopped and was facing him. "Luke," he finally said.

"Luke what?"

"Just Luke."

Gray nodded. "Do you need a place to stay for a few days, Luke?"

❧

*L*uke watched Gray move around the kitchen, his pace slow and sluggish. It was on the tip of his tongue to insist that the other man sit and take it easy while Luke fixed lunch but he remained silent. There'd been something in Gray's eyes after he'd introduced himself and shaken Luke's hand – a steely determination that made it seem like Gray had something to prove. That look and the strange sensation that had flickered beneath Luke's skin where their palms had connected had been preoccupying Luke's thoughts for the last fifteen minutes.

Saying yes to Gray's offer had been easy because Luke was simply out of options. He had less than twenty bucks in his wallet and absolutely nowhere to go.

"Turkey okay?"

"Yeah," Luke said absent-mindedly as he watched Gray rummaging through the fridge. He guessed them to be about the same size and

15

build but Gray had a certain rugged elegance to him. His coloring was unique too – dark blond hair that had a slight wave to it and was threaded with shades of caramel and copper. But it was Gray's eyes that had made something twist deep inside Luke. He'd seen hazel eyes on plenty of women but somehow none had ever seemed as beautiful as Gray's. Green along the outer edges that bled seamlessly into a soft shade of gold.

Luke knew it was fucked up to think of anything on the man as beautiful, especially his eyes, but it was even more fucked up that he'd hated seeing the flash of fear in Gray's gaze after Gray had stepped away from him while he'd been examining the injury he'd inflicted. It wasn't the first time Luke had seen that same expression but it was definitely the first time it had actually hurt.

"Sorry, it's not much," Gray said as he slid a sandwich piled high with turkey in front of Luke. "Haven't had time to shop yet this week." Gray's eyes shifted from his to the dog that was laying quietly at Luke's feet. "She have a name?" Gray asked as he began feeding the dog several slices of turkey.

Luke shook his head. "The piece of shit who was beating the hell out of her was calling her a worthless motherfucker so my guess is no, she doesn't. At least not one she should be stuck with for the rest of her life."

Gray's eyes lifted to meet his and another strange ache went through Luke. What the hell was wrong with him? He snatched up the sandwich and took a bite in an effort to distract himself.

"She's really not yours?" Gray asked.

Luke forced his eyes to the dog that was sitting politely at Gray's feet and carefully taking the proffered food. "Nope. I was walking past this old house and heard her yelping. I went to check it out and saw some old guy beating her with a 2 x 4. Fucker had her tied to a tree so she couldn't get away." Luke dropped his hand to the dog's head and stroked over it. "Always wanted a dog like this when I was a kid," he mused as the shepherd leaned against his leg while still taking the turkey from Gray.

"Looks like you got your wish," Gray said softly and Luke lifted his

16

eyes to meet Gray's. It took Luke a minute to find words. A flash of heat went down his spine and he actually had to break the eye contact.

"Right dog, wrong time," he murmured. "You've got a nice place here. Dog like this could keep an eye on things."

Several long seconds passed before he heard Gray answer. "Think on it," he said gently and then his big hand was skimming over the dog's muzzle, just inches from Luke's fingers. "That dog you wanted as a kid – you have a name picked out?"

"Ripley." At Gray's look of confusion Luke said, "You know, that badass chick from the *Alien* movies."

Gray shook his head. "Never saw them."

"Not even the first one?"

"I wasn't really a movie kind of kid. Books were more my thing." Gray glanced at the dog and smiled. "Ripley. It works," he added thoughtfully.

Luke forced his attention away from the warm smile that was still spread across Gray's features. "You're not eating?" he asked as he took another bite of his lunch.

Gray immediately went pale at the mention of food. "Uh, no," he said quickly.

"You should try to eat something...toast or soup if you have it."

Another shake of the head and then Gray closed his eyes. Luke quickly stood and put his sandwich on the kitchen counter so it would be out of Gray's line of sight. "You okay?" he asked as he settled a hand on Gray's shoulder. The other man's whole body was drawn tight with tension but he managed a nod and Luke settled back in his seat and waited. It was several minutes before Gray finally opened his eyes.

"Answer me one thing," Gray said and Luke stiffened but remained silent. "The gun...is it because you're military or because you need it?"

Luke studied Gray for a moment and then said, "Something tells me you already know the answer."

Gray was quiet for so long that Luke made a move to stand so he could gather his things to leave. But when Gray's fingers closed

17

around his wrist, he actually had to stifle a moan because he felt the touch everywhere.

"Just one more question," Gray said softly.

Luke was still reeling from the fact that this man's touch was fucking with his body so he just nodded.

"Will you please finish the bookshelf?"

∾

"Gray."

Gray opened his eyes as a heavy hand settled on his shoulder. It took him a moment to focus his gaze and when he did, he could see Luke's dark eyes watching him with concern.

"Sorry," Gray said as he struggled to sit up on the couch. "Guess I was more tired than I thought," he mumbled as he tried to ignore the exhaustion that continued to seep through him.

"Drink this," he heard Luke say a second before a bottle of water was thrust into his hand. The taste of metal immediately coated his tongue and he tried to hand the water back to Luke. "I'm okay."

"Drink it," Luke said again and Gray felt a shiver go through him at the rough order. It was on the tip of Gray's tongue to argue but then he looked down and saw the blanket draped across his lap – the one that hadn't been there when Gray had sat down on the couch to take a break from helping Luke construct the bookshelf. Not that he'd been helping much to begin with since he didn't know the first thing about building anything and he'd ended up spending most of his time watching Luke's powerful body flex and ripple as he'd painstakingly screwed the various pieces of wood together. It had been Luke who'd suggested he sit for a while and Gray could only assume it was because he'd started to look as off balance as he'd felt. The last thing he remembered was sinking into the smooth, soft cushions of the chocolate leather couch and watching Luke's big hands smoothing over the first shelf he'd attached to the branches that made up the side and back of the bookshelf.

Gray twisted the cap off the bottle and nearly shook his head at how worn out he felt just from doing that. He'd been expecting some fatigue but what he was feeling was off the charts. As expected, his first instinct when the water hit the back of his throat was to spit it out because it tasted so wrong but he closed his eyes and forced down several swallows. At least his stomach didn't protest and it was only that fact that had Gray sucking down a couple more pulls of the icy liquid before putting the cap back on the bottle. Luke, who was sitting on the coffee table in front of the couch, took the water from him and set it down on the end table.

"Keep drinking every few minutes. I'll get dinner started."

"Dinner?" Gray said in surprise and then he glanced out the window. Sure enough, it was pitch dark outside.

Luke stood and as soon as he stepped past the couch, Gray sucked in breath at the sight of the bookshelf that stood against the wall. "Luke, it's amazing," he said softly. The white bark stood in heavy contrast to the dark shelves and Gray struggled to his feet so he could get a closer look. A hand closed around his elbow to offer him support as he moved closer.

"Don't touch the shelves. They're still wet," he heard Luke say as Gray ran his fingers over one of the branches. The piece of furniture was so incredibly different than what Gray usually preferred but he found himself unable to take his eyes off of it.

"How did you do this?"

Luke was still holding his arm and Gray was torn between wanting to move away and stay exactly where he was. Since he was afraid he'd fall on his face without Luke's support, he didn't move.

"Just did. I found the stain in your shed...I hope you don't mind that I used it for this but I thought the darker shelves would look nice with the birch."

Gray glanced up at Luke. "I have a shed?"

Luke chuckled and the delicious sound slid over Gray.

"Out back. I guess you haven't lived here long?"

Gray shook his head and immediately regretted it because the move made him feel queasy. Luke must have sensed his discomfort because he led him back to the couch. "I bought this cabin a few years ago when I was looking for a place to get away to but this is the first time I've actually stayed here."

"Get away from what?" Luke asked as he draped the blanket back over Gray's lap.

"Life, I guess."

"But you never used it till now? How come?"

"Life, I guess," Gray said with a laugh.

"So you don't live here full-time?"

"No. L.A. – Malibu actually. What about you? Where are you from?" The questions were reasonable ones but as soon as he saw Luke's eyes drop, Gray knew they'd been the wrong ones. Of course the guy wasn't interested in sharing that kind of information about himself. He was clearly running from some serious shit.

"Georgia," Luke said softly. "Fort Benning."

Gray was caught off guard by the admission but decided not to press his luck with any more personal questions. And it absolutely wasn't because he wanted to reach out and run his fingers over Luke's cheek in the hopes of wiping away the haunted look that had over-taken his features. He was saved from having to say anything at all when he heard his cell phone ringing.

"I'll get it," Luke said quickly and then he was striding across the room and pulling Gray's phone from the desk drawer where he'd left it. He handed it to Gray and said, "I'm going to just go clean up outside."

Gray watched him leave through the front door before he glanced down at his phone. Dread went through him as he let his finger hover over the answer button but as another wave of exhaustion hit him, he pushed the red button instead and then dropped the phone onto the coffee table. He leaned back against the couch and let his eyes settle on the beautiful piece of furniture as his thoughts drifted to the mysterious man who'd created it.

∾

*S*tupid, stupid, stupid. What the hell had possessed him to tell Gray where he was from? All it would take was a Google search of his first name and Fort Benning and Gray would know exactly who he was.

Luke let out another rough curse as he threw the remaining pieces of wood debris onto the pile of firewood. He stalked back to the shed to grab the last few pieces of leftover wood and returned a moment later. His hands full, he came to a stop when he saw Gray watching him with concern.

"I heard something hit the house," Gray said quietly as he glanced at the pile of wood that had been neatly stacked against the side of the house but now had several pieces strewn all over the ground.

"Sorry," Luke mumbled as he placed the wood in his arms on the pile and then started reaching for the loose pieces. Gray helped him but Luke could see he was still unsteady on his feet and said, "Leave it. I'll take care of it."

Gray ignored him and continued to work but his moves were slow and Luke had nearly all the wood cleaned up by the time Gray reached for his third piece. Luke took it from him and put it on the pile.

"You're bleeding," he heard Gray whisper. "Again," he added and Luke dropped his eyes to his side and saw that blood was seeping through his shirt.

"It's nothing," Luke muttered.

"Come inside, let me take a look," Gray said but he didn't give Luke a chance to respond – he just turned and headed back into the cabin.

Luke entered the cabin and saw that Gray had pulled a kitchen chair away from the table. Although Gray wasn't around, Luke understood the message and dropped down into the chair and waited. Gray was back within a couple of minutes, his hands full of bandages and gauze.

Gray pulled out a chair and sat across from Luke. "Show me," he said as his eyes met Luke's. Something about the way Gray looked at him had Luke lifting his shirt. He kept his eyes on Gray as the other man began cleaning the injury and was surprised that not only was Gray not peppering him with questions about the wound, he wasn't flinching in the least as he mopped up the blood.

"Looks like you tore some stitches," Gray said.

Luke forced himself to look down and felt a sharp stab of something that wasn't pain go through him when Gray's thumb gently probed at the wound.

"I'm left handed so it's hard for me to reach that part," Luke said.

Gray's eyes lifted in surprise. "You stitched yourself up?"

Luke only nodded and he could see Gray's brain working but he still didn't ask the questions he clearly wanted to. "Do you think you could put a couple in there?" Luke asked.

Gray went pale at that but he hesitated for only a moment before he nodded. "If you tell me what to do."

"My kit's in my bag," Luke said as he glanced at the duffle sitting next to the couch.

Instead of looking through it, Gray brought the whole bag over and carefully settled it on Luke's lap. It took just a few seconds to locate his emergency medical kit. "It needs to be cleaned first."

Luke watched Gray intently as he got up to wash his hands and then prepare what he would need for the job. As exhausted as Gray looked, he remained steady on his feet and didn't actually look like he was going to pass out until Luke handed him the curved needle he would need to apply the stitches. By the time he explained the process, Gray had gone even paler than he already was.

"Gray, don't worry about it. I can manage-" Luke finally said as he reached for the needle.

"No, I'm okay," Gray said firmly and he closed his eyes and took a deep breath. "Just...just distract me, okay?"

It was on the tip of Luke's tongue to say that being distracted was the last thing Gray should be but when he saw the fear in Gray's eyes, he said, "Why books?"

"What?"

"You said you liked books instead of movies as a kid. Why?"

Gray's eyes shifted to his briefly but then he returned his attention to Luke's wound and forced the needle through Luke's skin. It hurt like hell but Luke managed to remain silent and Gray's look of concern had him sending the man a quick nod to indicate he was okay.

"Why books?" he prodded as the needle pierced his skin again.

"Something about being able to get lost in them I guess," Gray murmured.

"Did you need to get lost?"

Gray simply nodded.

"Why?"

Gray's eyes never left his work as he tied off the first stitch. "My parents fought a lot," was all he said.

"Are they still together?" Luke asked softly.

"Married forty-three years," Gray said solemnly.

"Happily?"

"If happily means they don't talk, sleep in separate rooms and my mom drinks herself into a stupor each night while my dad fucks an endless supply of mistresses, then yes, they're happy."

The hidden pain in Gray's voice had Luke wishing he could reach out and stroke the man's face. But since that was completely fucked up, he asked "What kind of books?" instead.

"Pretty much anything I could get my hands on. The classics – Steinbeck, Hemingway. Vonnegut was my hero."

"Is that why you became a writer?"

Gray stopped mid-stitch and looked up from what he was doing. "How did you know?"

Luke motioned to the open box of books in the corner of the living room. "I wanted to make sure the top of the bookshelf was strong enough to support your books so I grabbed a few from the box. You were asleep," he quickly added. "I saw your picture on the dust jacket of one of them."

Gray almost seemed disappointed by that and Luke felt a pang of guilt go through him though he wasn't sure what he should feel guilty for. "Gray-"

"How's that?" Gray asked as he tied off the last stitch. Luke looked down and saw that the edges of the wound were once again closed and the stitches Gray had put in looked surprisingly straight and tight.

"Perfect," Luke said. "Thank you."

"Well, you're a pretty good patient," Gray said lightly though the comment sounded forced and unnatural.

"Gray, I didn't mean to upset you…"

"You didn't," Gray said with a light smile but before he could stand, Luke snagged him by the wrist and pulled him back down so their knees were touching. He ignored the flash of heat that shot from his fingers down to his belly.

"Liar," Luke whispered.

Gray's eyes held his and then dropped to his mouth for the briefest of moments. It was enough to have Luke's whole body drawing up tight as his nerve endings began to sizzle with an undeniable reality. He wanted Gray.

The truth hit him so hard that Luke released Gray's arm and he leaned back in his chair to try and put as much distance between himself and the other man as he could. The move seemed to snap Gray out of his daze and he quickly stood and began cleaning up the bloodied gauze on the table.

"I think I'm going to skip dinner," Gray said. "This stomach flu is really kicking my ass. You can use the guest room next to mine or there's one at the end of the hallway."

"I'm actually going to head out," Luke murmured as he tracked Gray's movements throughout the kitchen.

"Okay," Gray said coolly as he began heading towards the hallway leading to the bedrooms but he stopped after just a few steps. He finally turned around and then took several steps until he was leaning heavily against the chair on the opposite side of the kitchen table. "I… I liked the idea that you didn't know who I was. It's been a while since I didn't have to worry about…"

Gray's voice dropped off and then his eyes fell to the floor. "I just wanted to help you, Luke, the way you helped me yesterday. You could have left me in that ditch. You could have cleaned me out after you got me back here. You could have done a whole lot of shit…guys like you don't exist in my world." Gray fell silent for a moment after that cryptic statement and then he finally pinned Luke with his gaze. "Whatever happened to you...you can trust me."

With that, Gray turned and left the room and Luke looked down at the wound. The jagged tear in his flesh was proof of what happened when you trusted the wrong person. So why then did he so badly want to believe the words when Gray said them?

CHAPTER 3

*"G*ray, wake up."

Gray tried to roll away from the hand that was shaking him gently but the hand wouldn't let him so he had no choice but to open his eyes. His gut clenched when he saw Luke sitting on the bed next to him, the curve of his ass actually brushing against Gray's hip through the light comforter. Luke's presence was surprise enough but his body's reaction was even more of one. While the most important part of his body might not be taking notice the way he would have liked, all the other tell-tale signs of desire that a beautiful man like Luke would stir in him were there – heated flesh, sweaty palms, increased breath.

"What is it? Is everything okay?" Gray asked and he quickly dropped his eyes to Luke's side to make sure his wound wasn't bleeding again. He never in his life wanted to have to put a needle through another person's skin but he'd do it in a heartbeat if that was what Luke needed.

"Everything's fine. You need to come eat."

"What?" Gray asked in astonishment. The man had woken him up for fucking food?

Gray forcibly rolled onto his side. "Not hungry," he muttered tiredly.

"When was the last time you ate?"

Gray tried to think back but his silence seemed to be the motivation Luke needed because suddenly he was being hauled to his feet. At least he'd had the sense to change into pajama bottoms yesterday before he'd crawled into his bed but he hadn't bothered with a shirt.

"Any nausea?" Luke asked as he began dragging Gray unceremoniously from the room. Ripley had been sitting next to Luke and pressed her cold nose against Gray's hand as he was pulled out of the room.

"Um, no," Gray said in surprise as he yanked his hand free of Luke's hold. The metallic taste was still in his mouth but it wasn't as prominent as before. He was about to tear Luke a new one for his high-handedness but his traitorous stomach chose that moment to growl.

A small smile caused the corners of Luke's mouth to pull up and Gray wanted to both kiss and punch the man at the same time. "Come on, I made eggs."

Gray was glad when Luke didn't reach for him again because one more touch and he probably would have gone with his first instinct to kiss him. He followed Luke to the kitchen and was surprised to see the table set with two places and a pile of eggs on each plate. There was also toast and coffee.

"You didn't have much in your fridge," Luke said as he went to the counter and grabbed the nearly empty container of milk off it.

Gray sat down and began picking at the food on his plate. As hungry as he was, his stomach still rolled at the sight of the scrambled eggs.

"Maybe just start with some toast?" Luke suggested.

"Yeah, maybe," Gray said and he watched as Luke swapped out the plates. Gray didn't put anything on the toast and was grateful it stayed down when he finally managed to swallow it. He and Luke ate in silence for several moments and when Luke finished the last of his food, he got up and pulled a bottle of water from the fridge. Gray wasn't surprised when Luke put it down in front of him instead of keeping it for himself.

"I didn't hurt anyone," Luke suddenly blurted out and Gray stopped mid-chew to stare at him. "And I only pointed the gun at you because I was confused – I guess the heat made me pass out...that's how I ended up in that ditch. And then you were grabbing me. I just reacted."

Gray swallowed down the rest of the food in his mouth and then took a drag on the water. "Someone's after you?"

Luke nodded. His lack of any additional explanation had Gray scrapping his instinct to ask who. "How did you end up here?"

"I thought a friend of mine lived out here but he doesn't anymore."

Gray could tell that wasn't the entire story but instead of calling Luke on it, he asked, "Don't you have any family? Other friends? Wife or girlfriend?"

A shake of the head. "I grew up in group homes mostly. A couple foster homes too. And being deployed almost non-stop for ten years isn't exactly a selling point when it comes to women who are looking to settle down and start a family." A shadow passed over Luke's features when he said, "My only friends were the guys in my unit."

Which meant those guys were either gone or they were the reason he was on the run.

"Gray, I have no idea who you are other than you wrote a book. I thought about Googling you last night but I didn't. Maybe you're not on the run like me but I'm guessing you're running from something."

The truth of Luke's statement hit Gray hard. He hadn't considered his escape from his life in L.A. in that way but in a sense, it was true.

"If the offer to stay here for a bit still stands, I'd like to take you up on it. I don't think the people looking for me will be able to track me here but if things get too hot, I'll go. I won't put you in danger."

A strange, warm sensation built in Gray's stomach at Luke's adamant declaration but he shook it off and focused on forcing another piece of toast into his system. "The offer stands. For as long as you need it."

"One more thing," Luke said as he leaned forward. "I need to carry my own weight around here. I'm pretty good with my hands so if there's something you need done…"

Gray's eyes shifted to Luke's big hands and he felt his mouth go dry. He had to suck down more water to get the bread to go down.

"Um, yeah, I was actually thinking about doing some remodeling. I was going to hire somebody…"

"Great," Luke said with a wide smile that had Gray's insides knotting up. Fuck, this was so incredibly bad.

~

"Oh God, I think I'm going to be sick," Luke heard Gray mutter but a quick glance showed that the man's round eyes were still focused on the television screen. His expression was a mix of horror and awe.

"I know, it's awesome, right?" Luke said as he watched the alien rip its way from the man's stomach. "*Alien* in high def is definitely the way to go," he said with a chuckle.

"How did I not see this movie?" Gray asked hoarsely when the gruesome scene ended. He dropped his hand to rest on the dog that was laying stretched out between them on the couch. Luke had been surprised when Gray had invited Ripley up onto the expensive looking piece of furniture but as he watched Gray's hand gently drag back and forth over the animal's fur, he actually felt a twinge of jealousy.

Jesus, three days in the man's company and Luke was a fucking mess. He was nearly thirty years old, had been with his fair share of women and had spent the better part of his life around strong, confident, and what even he as a straight man would deem good looking men. Not once had he even felt a hint of attraction towards any of them. Hell, even his openly gay foster brother whom he'd first met at the age of sixteen had failed to elicit even the slightest stirring of anything but friendship. But the pull Gray had on him was slowly driving him insane. Every time he looked at Gray or even just heard the silky, smooth way Gray said his name, his cock swelled to life and images of him sliding into Gray's welcoming heat had Luke retreating outside or to another room. On several occasions, he'd even resorted to jacking off just so he could be in the man's presence long enough to talk about some of the remodeling ideas he had.

"Luke."

It took Luke a moment to realize Gray was talking to him and it took everything in him to drag his eyes from the long, thick fingers still sifting through Ripley's fur. What would they feel like wrapped around his cock? Would his grip be stronger than a woman's? Rougher? Would he know exactly how much pressure to exert to drive Luke insane with pleasure?

"Luke!"

"What?" he said as he snapped his eyes up.

Gray laughed. "Would you pause it for a second?" he asked as he motioned to the movie and then to the remote in Luke's hand. The remote he'd been stroking with his thumb as an image of Gray's lips hovering just over his had assailed him.

"Yeah," Luke bit out as he tried to shift his weight to give himself some much needed room in his pants. Unfortunately, Ripley's big head was resting on his gut and while the dog's position hid his growing erection from Gray, it did nothing to help ease the discomfort Luke was feeling.

"You want something to drink?" Gray asked as he pulled himself to his feet. Although the man finally seemed to be on the mend, he continued to move slowly as if he were in constant pain and Luke had caught him nodding off more than once during lulls in conversation or when he'd sat down on the couch to take a breather.

"No, thanks," he said as he used his hand to ease Ripley's head off his body. But before he could do much, the dog suddenly tensed and then growled. Luke was already reaching for the gun he'd put on the coffee table as Ripley flew off the couch and began barking at the front door.

"Get to your room," Luke snapped at Gray. "Lock the door!"

Luke was striding for the front door when Gray suddenly stepped in front of him. "Luke, take it easy. It's probably nothing," Gray said softly as his hand pressed against Luke's chest. The touch did nothing to ease Luke's tension and he quickly moved past Gray and glanced through the space between the curtains on a side window. The sight of a police car parked in front of Gray's truck had his brain going into overdrive. He sensed Gray behind him and he spun around.

"Your room, now!" he bit out. "If this ends bad, tell them I was holding you hostage," he added quickly as he reached over to the door and flipped the deadbolt. It wouldn't buy him a lot of time but enough that he might be able to make it to the line of trees behind the cabin. That was assuming no one was covering the back door.

"Damn it, Luke, look at me!" Gray snapped. Luke was so distracted, he was caught off guard when Gray's hands closed around his upper arms and shoved him against the wall.

A knock rattled the front door. "Gray, it's Jax!" a voice called out.

"He's a friend," Gray quickly said but his eyes never left Luke's. "Trust me," he added. "Please."

Luke fought every instinct to force Gray to release him. He finally managed a curt nod and eased his finger from the trigger of the gun.

"Stay in your room," Gray said. "I'll take care of this."

Fuck, why didn't the guy just ask him to stop breathing too?

"Luke," Gray repeated softly. Just hearing the pleading in Gray's voice was enough to get Luke moving. But he didn't go to his room – he stopped in the hallway just beyond the kitchen where he'd be out of sight but he'd be able to hear every word spoken and he'd still have a chance to get away if Gray ended up turning on him just like all the others had.

～

"*R*ipley, quiet," Gray ordered as he unlocked the door. Adrenaline was still surging through his system at the near miss. Luke had shifted so quickly from someone who'd been completely relaxed to someone fully prepared to defend himself that it had taken Gray several long seconds to catch up.

"Deputy Reid," Gray said in greeting as he opened the door.

Jaxon Reid was the kind of guy you knew not to fuck with just by looking at him but that didn't stop Gray from adding a drawl to his words that belied the tension running through his system. "If you wanted to take me up on my dinner invitation, you could have asked Dane to call me. He and I haven't had a chance to chat much."

Jax's eyes narrowed and Gray had to bite back a smile. He'd gotten off on the wrong foot with Jax from day one when he'd met and struck up a conversation with Jax's boyfriend in Dare's only bookstore. Jax had made it clear that Gray wasn't welcome when the kindhearted country vet, Dane Winters, who'd also turned out to be a fan of Gray's books, had invited him to dinner. Gray had been attracted to Dane from the get go but he hadn't missed the way the two men had looked at each other. Not to mention that Gray hadn't been in the market for a boyfriend or even a quick fuck so his attraction hadn't been something he would have acted on anyway. He'd been all set to decline the dinner invitation when Jax had bulldozed his way into the conversation and uninvited Gray. It had been a challenge that Gray just couldn't pass on. The dinner had been rife with tension and in the following weeks there'd been a point where some pretty serious shit had gone down between Jax and Dane but the pair had managed to work it out and Gray hadn't been surprised to learn that the big man was back in town and that he'd signed on as a deputy in the Dare Police Department. He'd also shacked up with the good looking vet and his adorable baby girl.

"Gray," Jax muttered in greeting. "I'm afraid this is official business," he said quietly. "May I come in?"

Gray tensed and gently closed his hand over the scruff of Ripley's neck to pull the dog back. Luckily the dog wasn't acting aggressively anymore and when Jax put out his hand to let the dog sniff it, Ripley wagged her tail.

"What's up, Deputy?" Gray said lightly.

"Do you know Otis Lister?"

"That old guy that runs the junkyard outside town?" Gray asked. He'd driven by the dilapidated property dozens of times on his way to the city, but hadn't noticed much about it other than it was full of rusted out cars and farm equipment and there were piles of scrap metal all over the place. He'd never met or even seen the old man who owned the place but had heard enough stories from people in town that the guy was a mean son of a bitch who wasn't above pointing his shotgun at anyone who accused him of giving them a raw deal. "Never met him," Gray said.

"He came into the station a few days ago to report that someone assaulted him and stole his dog," Jax said and Gray stiffened when Jax's gaze slid to Ripley. "One of his neighbors mentioned seeing a dog fitting the description of Lister's dog in your driveway while he was driving past on the way to his hunting spot."

Fuck.

"I took the dog," Gray quickly said. "I heard Lister beating the shit out of it as I was driving by his place."

Jax's face fell and Gray was surprised to see what looked like disappointment in his expression. Before he could say anything else, Gray saw Jax's hand rest on the butt of his gun as his eyes looked beyond Gray's shoulder to a spot behind him and his stomach dropped out when he turned to see Luke studying them both. Thankfully, the gun was nowhere to be seen but Gray suspected it wasn't too far out of reach.

Gray could tell Luke was about to say something so he quickly turned his attention back to Jax. "Do you need me to come down to the station with you?"

"Gray..." Luke began.

"It's okay, baby, I won't be gone long," Gray said as he cast a too bright smile over his shoulder at Luke. He hoped to God the man could see his unspoken warning to keep his mouth shut. He turned his attention back to Jax and quipped, "They get attached so quickly – even the one-nighters." A flash of something went through Jax's expression but Gray ignored it. Jax's eyes shifted once more to Luke and then his hard gaze settled on Gray.

"I'm going to need to take the dog with me," Jax said quietly.

"No," Luke said, his tone lethal. Jax stiffened and Gray felt the situation spiraling out of control as Luke came up behind him. Gray kept his eyes on Jax as he reached behind him and settled his hand on what turned out to be Luke's stomach. His hope was to both silence Luke and to convince Jax that Luke was simply an overexcited lover.

"Jax," Gray said quietly in an effort to get the man's attention back on him.

Jax's eyes returned to him. "I need to take the dog so Dane can examine her, Gray. She'll be safe with us tonight."

Gray felt Luke's body tighten beneath his palm but thankfully, he remained quiet.

"And Lister?"

Jax didn't answer. Instead he said, "Don't leave town." But Gray had the sneaking suspicion he wasn't saying it to him. Jax opened the door. "Come on, girl," he said to the dog.

"Ripley," Gray said. "Her name is Ripley."

But the dog had already trotted out the door. Jax gave him and Luke another quick look and then he was gone, pulling the door shut behind him. Luke instantly stepped away from him and Gray felt a pang of loss go through him.

"You shouldn't have done that," Luke ground out as he went to look out the window. Gray's heart nearly stopped when he saw the clear outline of Luke's gun tucked in the waistband of his jeans. He'd had the sense to cover the gun with his shirt but if he'd turned his back even once to Jax, the sharp eyed cop would have seen it.

"It was the only thing I could think of to explain your presence," Gray said wearily. "Besides, Jax is gay too so he won't think anything of it. And with my reputation-"

"What the hell are you talking about?" Luke snapped in obvious irritation. He was so wound up that he kept clenching and unclenching his fingers.

"Luke, I'm sorry if I offended you by letting Jax believe you were gay but it was the only way-"

"I don't give a fuck about that," Luke nearly yelled as he suddenly got in Gray's face. Gray actually backed up until his back hit the door but Luke just closed the distance between them, his eyes glittering with anger. "You shouldn't have taken the fall for me!"

"What?"

"I was handling it!"

Fury went through Gray and he shoved Luke hard until the man had no choice but to back up a couple of steps to maintain his balance. "Handling it? Is that what you call it? What was your grand plan? Shoot your way out of here? He's a fucking police officer, Luke, not to mention my friend! Are you telling me you would have shot him?"

When Luke didn't answer him, a rush of doubt went through Gray. God, had he really gotten this all wrong? Had he just stuck his neck out for a cold-blooded killer instead of a good man who'd gotten caught up in some pretty bad shit?

Luke's silence was so unnerving that Gray felt an overwhelming need to escape. But he only made it a couple of steps before Luke's hand closed around his arm.

"I wouldn't have hurt him," Luke said in a rush. "I need you to believe that."

The words alone weren't enough to convince Gray but the desperation in Luke's voice was. Gray managed a nod but when Luke continued to hold on to him, Gray's anxiety turned into something else. Something he shouldn't be feeling – not around this man...not around any man.

"You need to tell him the truth tomorrow."

Gray extricated himself from the fingers that were starting to burn his skin. "No," he said simply. "I can deal with the fallout."

"I don't want you fighting my battles."

"And you're not putting yourself at risk just because you did the right thing," Gray snapped. "At most I'll get a slap on the wrist. And that's assuming my very expensive lawyers don't get the charges dropped before the ink even dries on the paperwork."

Luke looked like he wanted to say something else but he only hardened his jaw and then turned and disappeared down the back hallway. A door slammed shut a second later. Gray felt a wave of exhaustion pass through him as the adrenaline in his system began to wane and it took everything in him to make it to the couch before his legs gave out. The movie was still on pause on the TV but the idea of watching it without Luke didn't appeal to him so Gray reached for the remote that had gotten stuck between the couch cushions and shut it off. He stared at the black screen for a long time before his eyes grew heavy; he used his last reserves of energy to stumble his way to his bedroom.

CHAPTER 4

"How is she?" Gray asked as soon as he stepped out of his truck. He'd debated calling Dane to ask about Ripley but had decided to make the drive to the vet's house instead after his less than friendly encounter with Luke this morning. Gray had actually assumed Luke would take off at some point in the dead of night and he'd confirmed that fact by peering into the empty guest bedroom that looked as unused as the day he'd offered it to Luke. It wasn't until he'd heard the rhythmic sound of a hammer striking wood above his head that Gray had realized Luke was still around, but had retreated to the roof to start patching the holes he'd mentioned to Gray the day after he'd insisted on pulling his weight. Gray had gone outside to say good morning but the icy glare that Luke had shot him had had Gray storming back into the house to grab his car keys.

"Come see for yourself," Dane said from where he stood at the top of the stairs leading into the quaint Victorian style home. It had been a while since he'd seen Dane but Gray could tell that finding the love of his life had done a world of good for the other man. He looked...at peace.

"You feeling okay, Gray? You look a little pale," Dane commented as he followed Dane inside.

"Just getting over the flu," he hedged. To change the subject, he said, "The walking steroid around?"

"You do realize you and Jax are pretty much the same size, right?" Dane said with a laugh.

Gray did know that, but something about Jax's presence always made him seem bigger, more commanding.

"Jax had an errand to run," Dane was saying as he pulled the door closed. "She's in here."

He followed Dane to the kitchen and couldn't help but smile when he saw Ripley lying on the floor beneath Dane's daughter's high chair. The big dog was trying to lick what looked like baby food off her muzzle but couldn't quite reach it. Emma had her head craned over the side so she could see the dog and kept dropping more baby food all over the floor and the dog.

"Hey, Ripley," Gray called and the dog quickly jumped up and came to greet him. Gray wiped the baby food off the dog's face and let her lick the remnants from his finger. "So what's the verdict?" Gray asked as he skimmed his hand over the dog's too thin body.

Dane's expression darkened at the question but he schooled his features so as not to upset his daughter as he began the task of cleaning up her breakfast. "Lister did a number on her. She's under-weight by about twenty pounds and from the condition of her skin and coat, she's malnourished too. I was able to get some X-rays last night when Jax brought her home. I counted at least six cracked ribs that had healed over and two fresh ones. You can't see it because of her fur, but her body is covered in scars which makes me think Lister hit her with something sharp – since the guy runs a scrapyard, it could have been just about anything."

Gray's heart broke for the dog. "Any idea how old she is?"

"Between two and three."

Gray shook his head. "Bastard," he muttered under his breath.

"At least you got her out of there," Dane added as he pulled Emma out of the high chair. Gray wasn't particularly comfortable with taking credit for rescuing the dog but he also knew that anything he said to Dane would make it back to Jax.

"You'll make sure he doesn't get her back, right Dane?" Gray asked as he rose to his feet.

Before Dane could answer, the front door opened and Jax walked in. Emma began clapping her hands excitedly and Gray swore he heard her say what sounded like "Papa."

Jax gave him a quick nod as he strode past and then he was gathering his daughter in his arms.

"Morning, baby girl," he crooned before leaning down to seal his lips over Dane's. "Morning," he said huskily.

The scene was so sweetly domestic that Gray felt his chest constrict and he had to drop his eyes back down to where Ripley was leaning against his leg. A family wasn't something he'd ever imagined wanting for himself but now...well, now it didn't matter because it was too late.

"Coffee, Gray?" he heard Jax ask and was surprised to look up and find that it was just the two of them in the kitchen.

"No, thanks," he said. "I've put a call in to my attorney this morning but since he's on Pacific time, he probably won't be getting back to me for a bit. He'll want to be present when I'm questioned."

Jax studied him for a long moment as he sipped his coffee. "That won't be necessary," he finally said. "Lister won't be pressing charges. He's also relinquished ownership of the dog so you can take her home."

Gray couldn't hide his shock. "Just like that?"

"Just like that."

Jax's knowing gaze was making him uncomfortable so he turned to leave but he only made it a couple of steps before curiosity overcame him and he turned back. "How?"

Jax seemed to know what he was talking about because he said, "I had a long chat with Lister this morning." Jax's demeanor was so calm and relaxed that it had Gray on edge. "I suggested he might want to rethink pressing charges and that maybe owning any kind of pet in the future wasn't a great idea."

Gray would have smiled at that if he hadn't been so preoccupied with what Jax wasn't saying. "Why?"

If the one word questions bothered Jax, he didn't show it. But he also didn't answer, so Gray said, "For Dane?" It was the only reasonable explanation. No way would Jax have gone to bat for Gray – it just didn't compute. The man hated him.

"No, not for Dane," Jax said as he refilled his coffee. "Why don't you stay for some breakfast, Gray?"

"Um, I've got to get back," Gray said. He'd like to think the excuse was about Luke but in truth, the conversation with Jax was fucking with his head. The guy was being too nice and that always meant one thing...he wanted something. "Thanks," Gray mumbled as he turned to leave.

"Gray."

Gray stiffened and forced himself to turn around. Here it was – the favor, the request...whatever it was that Jax wanted in return for his assistance.

"Next time, have your story straight before you take the blame for something," Jax said softly. "The speed limit on the road going past Lister's place is 55 – no way you would have heard that dog from your truck at that speed."

Heat went through Gray. So Jax had known all along. And he hadn't called him out on the lie...

Gray wasn't sure if he managed a nod or not as he turned and left the house. Ripley followed him without any prompting which was strangely comforting since he'd already found himself getting attached to the dog. Only problem was, he was getting attached to the dog's new owner just as quickly.

～

*L*uke heard the truck approaching but only glanced up from the hole he was patching on the roof long enough to confirm it was Gray's. He wasn't surprised when there was no greeting this time around – just the slamming of the front door. It was exactly what he deserved considering his behavior the night before. If he'd had any sense, he would have tried to explain to Gray the abject fear that had gone through him when he'd heard the car rolling up Gray's driveway last night. He hadn't even had time to consider how he'd been found because his first thought was to protect the man who'd offered him sanctuary. His next thought had been about escape. And then Gray had gone and done it again – asked him to trust him for the second time. Hiding had gone against every one of Luke's instincts but he'd done it anyway. And then that fucking lie about the dog had spilled from Gray's lips and the combination of shock and anger that had rolled through Luke had him stepping around the doorframe and into the kitchen. He'd locked eyes with the cop instantly and hadn't missed the way the man's hand had gone to his gun. He also hadn't missed the look of fear on Gray's face when he'd seen Luke.

A high pitch bark distracted Luke from his thoughts and he glanced down and saw Ripley staring up at him, her big tail wagging back and forth in excitement. An unexpected rush of happiness went through Luke at the sight of the dog followed by the unhappy realization that he'd already become more attached to the animal than he would have liked. As Ripley's barks increased and she began bouncing up and down on her front legs, Luke smiled and made his way to the ladder that was propped along the side of the cabin. By the time his boots hit the ground, Ripley was all over him.

"Hey girl," he said as he patted the dog's side. He glanced at the cabin and knew it was time to stop putting off the inevitable conversation he needed to have with Gray. As he made his way towards the door, his gut clenched much like it had last night when Gray had put his palm against his stomach. Luke had known the move was just to convince the cop that he and Gray had something going on between them but fuck, that touch had sent shockwaves through his entire system and he'd gotten instantly hard. He hadn't cared one whit that Gray had insinuated Luke was gay but learning that Gray was had opened up a whole new world of images and thoughts for Luke. The fantasies he'd had about Gray had somehow seemed more like a possibility if he could just get past the weirdness of being suddenly attracted to another man for the first time in his life.

Luke went into the cabin and found Gray sitting at the kitchen table, his big hands wrapped around a cup of coffee.

"Hey," Luke said as he closed the door and shrugged off the light jacket he'd been wearing. Although it was late summer, the mornings were still chilly in the Montana mountains.

Gray ignored him and stared out the window.

"You hungry?" Luke asked as went to the fridge and pulled out the nearly empty carton of eggs.

"No."

"Gray, you need-"

"To eat, I know," Gray said coolly. "Tell you what, Luke. You don't want me fighting your battles, I don't want you fighting mine. So how about we just stay out of each other's way?" Gray snapped as he stood and headed towards his bedroom.

"Gray, I'm sorry," Luke said as he shoved the carton of eggs away and followed Gray. He nearly slammed into the other man as soon as he rounded the corner because Gray had stopped moving.

"Save your apologies. Lister's not pressing charges so your conscience is clear. Stay, go, I don't give a shit," Gray snapped before he stormed into his room and shut the door in Luke's face.

Frustration went through Luke and he threw the door open but froze when he saw Gray in the process of stripping off his shirt. The sight of firm, tanned flesh had Luke coming to a stop. It wasn't the first time he was seeing Gray's body since he'd helped the man change into sweats and a T-shirt the night after they'd met but considering how sick Gray had been, Luke hadn't really taken the time to study or appreciate the man's wide shoulders, defined muscles and narrow waist. The only thing that would make the sight any better was if the pants went next but Gray had stopped unbuttoning them when he'd heard the door open.

"Like what you see?" he heard Gray drawl. Luke knew the words were meant to make him uncomfortable but he couldn't help but wonder what Gray would do if he said yes. Or better yet, if he walked up to Gray and finished the job of taking his pants off for him.

His silence seemed to set Gray off further because the man shook his head and began moving towards his bathroom. Luke knew he should just go. Pack what little shit he had and get his ass back on the road. He could figure out all the rest later. But hadn't this place been what he was looking for when he'd come to Montana? Hadn't he hoped to find someone he could trust – who'd have his back when he needed it most? No, he hadn't imagined it would be a virtual stranger but how many men would have done for him what Gray had done last night?

"The cops think I killed someone."

~

*G*ray stopped just before he reached the bathroom. He'd known whatever Luke was hiding was bad but he sure as hell hadn't expected the man to actually tell him the truth.

"I didn't do it," Luke quickly added.

"I believe you," Gray automatically said. And he did. God help him, he had no idea why his gut was telling him to trust this man but it was. He turned to face Luke and saw him still standing near the door, his frame stiff and unyielding.

"Someone I trusted set me up…did this," Luke said as he pointed to the injury on his side. "It's safer if you don't know the details."

Gray couldn't help but wonder if Luke was hesitant to tell him everything because he still didn't trust him. But that was irrelevant so he said, "I can get you the best lawyers. I know Jax will help too – I think he used to be FBI…"

Luke shook his head but didn't say anything.

"Okay," Gray said softly. "Tell me what you need, Luke."

A haunted look passed over Luke's features before he schooled them. "This, Gray. Exactly what you're doing. That's what I need."

Gray wanted to say that he could do more but he could already see Luke withdrawing so he nodded. "For as long as you need it."

~

"Where'd you learn to do this?" Gray asked as he tried to tear his eyes from Luke's ass as he bent over the piece of flooring he'd just knocked into place.

"A guy I met during boot camp started up a contracting business when he finished his deployment. I used to help out in my down time."

"Was that the kind of work you wanted to do when you got out?" Gray asked.

Luke sat back on his heels and wiped his arm across his forehead. "No, I was a lifer."

"A lifer?"

"I knew from the second I enlisted that I was exactly where I was supposed to be. I figured I'd become an instructor or something once I got to the point that I couldn't serve on the front lines anymore."

Gray lowered himself to the floor and leaned back against the wall. "What made you enlist?"

Luke took a long drink from the bottle of water Gray had brought him. "My foster brother was planning to join. He was the closest thing to family I had and I didn't want to lose him so I did too."

"Are you guys still in touch?"

Like shook his head. "We did two tours together but he had his heart set on joining the police academy and I had a chance to become a Ranger so we just kind of lost touch when we went our separate ways."

"You're an Army Ranger?"

A darkness settled over Luke's features but he nodded.

"You love it," Gray said softly.

Another nod.

"Why?"

Luke was quiet for a long time and Gray wished he had the right to lean over and brush his lips over Luke's in an attempt to offer comfort.

"It was the first time my life had purpose," Luke finally said. "And the first time I was ever really good at something."

"I don't believe that," Gray whispered.

Luke chuckled. "It's true. I was a lousy student...only reason I even graduated was because Rhys used to tutor me."

"Is Rhys your foster brother?"

Luke's eyes snapped up and Gray realized he hadn't been aware that he'd let the name slip. "Yeah."

"He's who you came out here to see, isn't he?" Gray said. "He's a deputy in the Dare police department."

Luke swallowed hard. "I saw the story in the news about him – about how he was wrongly sent to prison back in Chicago. It said he was working on a ranch outside Dare."

Gray was familiar with the story and had met Rhys Tellar only briefly before he'd signed on to be one of the town's deputies. Rhys had arrived in Montana a couple months earlier and had become involved in a relationship with Callan Bale, the owner of the CB Bar Ranch, and his young ranch hand, Finn Stewart.

"Were you headed to his ranch the day we met?"

"I was on my way back to town from the ranch. I didn't know Rhys had joined the police department out here. I saw him pull into the driveway in his police cruiser and I knew...I knew he couldn't help me."

"He didn't see you?"

"No. I was watching from some trees across the road from the ranch's driveway."

Gray felt a surge of pity go through him. It was clear that Rhys had been Luke's last hope. "Luke, Rhys seems like a pretty good guy...I'm sure he'd help you in any way he could."

Luke shook his head slowly. "I can't put him in that position. He's finally in a good place – I'm not going to fuck with that."

"Luke-"

"We should get this finished," Luke said as he turned his attention back to the floor.

∾

"*I*'m going to be gone for a couple days," Luke heard Gray say over the sound of the running faucet. "I've got some business in the city tomorrow afternoon and it'll just be easier to spend the night. I should be back on Wednesday sometime."

"Okay," Luke murmured as he put the last of the dishes on the counter next to the sink. "I'll get that dishwasher installed."

"Great," Gray said non-committedly. He didn't even look up from what he was doing.

It had been this way for three days – the stunted conversation, the overly polite greetings, the long drags of uncomfortable silence. And it was entirely Luke's fault. He'd felt raw and vulnerable after admitting why he'd come to Montana and even more so that he'd said Rhys' name without even realizing it. Somehow in the span of a week, Gray Hawthorne had managed to tie him up in knots both physically and emotionally. So he'd done the only thing he could think of and shut down in the hopes that Gray wouldn't pry any more information from him. And Gray had gotten the message pretty quickly and hadn't spoken to him beyond complimenting the finished hardwood floor in the living room and thanking him for fixing the leaky faucet in the master bathroom.

"I'm going to take Ripley outside for a few," he said quietly.

No response.

Once he was outside, Luke felt all his frustration well to the surface and he just started walking towards the back of the property. It was dark out but the full moon that sat heavy in the cloudless sky made it possible for him to find his way to the small creek that was nestled just beyond the tree line. Ripley dashed through the water happily while Luke dropped down to sit on the fallen tree that was just feet from the water's edge. Within minutes, the chilly air had the desired effect and he felt the anxiety in his gut ease. But it wouldn't completely go away and he knew while he was around Gray that it probably never would. Even if he looked past the growing physical attraction that he was struggling with, he couldn't ignore the fact that he was drawn to Gray in a way he hadn't been to any of the men in his unit or even Rhys when they'd been kids. And none of it made any sense because he'd known the man for less than a week.

Maybe Gray leaving for a couple of days would be a good thing – the week had been a roller coaster of highs and lows and it was likely just the stress that was playing havoc with his emotions and his body. But as Luke began walking back to the cabin, he couldn't help but wonder what kind of business Gray had in the city. He and Gray had already driven to Missoula twice this week to get remodeling supplies from one of the large home improvement warehouses and one of the first things Luke had noticed was the way Gray carried himself in public. He often kept his sunglasses on and constantly checked their surroundings as if expecting someone to be following them. If Luke hadn't known better, he would have thought Gray was the one on the run. Maybe the guy had a stalker or something…it wasn't something Luke would have thought writers would have but what the hell did he know?

Which was why it was all the more strange that Gray would be returning to the city for an extended period of time. An ugly thought filtered through Luke's brain as he remembered the insinuation that Gray had made to the cop about Luke's presence – like he was just some random guy Gray had picked up. Gray had mentioned something about having a reputation. What if he was going to Missoula to hook up? Luke doubted there were a lot of options for Gray in the small town of Dare. The idea had acid burning through Luke's gut and all the tension he'd managed to work off with his walk came screaming back. God, this really was fucked up. He wanted Gray even though he didn't want to. He felt connected to Gray even though he didn't want to be. He trusted Gray even though he shouldn't.

Luke let himself back into the quiet cabin. The only light on was the one over the sink in the kitchen, a clear sign that Gray had gone to bed despite the early hour. As much as Luke's brain was telling him to throw Gray's door open and confront him about why he was going to the city, Luke ignored it and went to his own room. He took a quick shower and then crawled into bed. Hours passed as he tried to seek the comfort of sleep and when he heard the bedroom door next to his open and close in the early hours the next morning, he barely kept himself from jumping out of bed so that he could hunt Gray down and tell him everything he was looking for was right under his nose. But he waited until he heard the sound of Gray's diesel engine roaring to life before he sat up and swung his legs over the bed. His cock was tight with need against his abdomen and within seconds of stepping under shower's hot water, he was pulling an epic climax from his body as he imagined what it would feel like to sink into Gray as the other man whispered his name.

He spent the rest of the day installing the dishwasher Gray had bought earlier in the week on their second trip to Missoula. But it wasn't until that night that he was plagued with more thoughts of Gray and his faceless lover and no amount of walking through the darkened woods brought him any relief. Even Ripley's antics failed to elicit any kind of response and he ended up tackling the chore of re-facing Gray's kitchen cabinets at three o' clock in the morning. It was a task that Gray had only mentioned that he was considering but since Luke had nothing else to keep him from going insane with jealousy, he ended up ripping all the doors off and emptying the cabinets so he could begin the process of stripping and sanding them. It wasn't until almost lunch time the next day that he'd been too exhausted to continue and he'd fallen asleep on the couch. It was dark when he heard tires on the driveway and a mix of apprehension and pleasure went through him at the same time when he heard the diesel engine. Ripley took off out the door as soon as Luke opened it but one look at Gray and all of Luke's excitement turned to concern as he saw Gray's stiff gait and careful movements.

"Gray?" Luke called as he hurried outside and reached for Gray's arm.

Gray shook him off and said, "Sorry I'm so late. There was an accident and the highway was shut down for hours. I'm really beat..."

Luke glanced at his watch and saw that it was well past dinner time. He trailed Gray into the cabin but Gray didn't stop moving as he walked past the disaster zone that used to be his kitchen nor did he comment at the sight of dishes piled everywhere and all the doors laying on top of each other on the kitchen table.

"Gray, are you sick again?" Luke asked as he finally got a look at Gray's features in the light of the cabin. His face was ashen and there were dark bags under his eyes. His lips looked dry and chapped and he had his hand clenched around his coat lapels as if trying to hold it closed to keep the cold out.

Gray shook his head. "Went out for a few drinks last night...well, maybe more than a few," Gray said cheekily. "Night."

The statement was like a slap in the face and Luke couldn't force himself to follow Gray to his room. So Gray *had* gone to Missoula to meet someone. It was what Luke had suspected all along so why did hearing the truth of it hurt so damn bad? Fury tore through Luke and before he could stop himself, he slammed his hand against the wall by the hallway that led to the bedrooms. Pain tore through his hand but he welcomed it as he spun on his heel and left the cabin.

$\approx$

*G*ray had no idea what the thumping sound somewhere outside his bedroom was but he was too tired to care as he sank down onto his bed. His whole body hurt as he tried to toe off his shoes and he finally gave up and slowly lay back on the bed and closed his eyes. It probably would have been smart to spend another night at the motel in Missoula but he'd already been on edge with staying in the city for nearly two days. He knew it wasn't realistic to think the paparazzi would find him clinging to the toilet bowl in some run-down motel on the outskirts of the city but it wasn't the first time his paranoia had gotten the better of him. After all, he'd seen firsthand what the self-proclaimed reporters were capable of. But as much as he would have liked his fear of the press to be his only reason for coming home sooner than he should have, Gray knew it was a big fat fucking lie. From the second he'd left the cabin yesterday morning, he'd been driving himself crazy wondering if Luke would still be here when he got back. It shouldn't have mattered whether the man had left or not considering how chilly things had been between them but it had mattered. More than Gray wanted it to.

While his continued attraction to Luke wasn't a surprise, it was how much he'd started enjoying the man's company that had caught him off guard. With his nose buried in books most of the time in grade and high school, Gray hadn't managed to secure his place in any of the social circles at school. And he'd been okay with that. College hadn't been much different since he'd spent what little free time he had writing and it hadn't taken him long after he'd sold the first million copies of his book to realize that all the so called friends that came out of the woodwork were nothing more than trolls hoping to spend a little time in the spotlight that had glared down on him so brightly.

But it hadn't meant that Gray couldn't have a little bit of fun with his newfound fame which had taken on a life of its own after he'd come out in a well-known magazine's feature article. For someone who'd been invisible for most of his life, he'd taken full advantage of the play-boy reputation his publicists had suggested. A team of stylists, a personal trainer and buckets of cash had meant he could have his pick of men. Groupies, wanna-be celebrities, it didn't matter. Hell, he'd even managed to bag himself some closeted A-listers who walked the red carpet with their supermodel girlfriends or actress wives and then secreted themselves away with him in some remote motel where he'd fuck them until they couldn't remember their own names. Then he'd had the pleasure of brushing elbows with them at some event or fundraiser and he'd see the flash of fear in their eyes as they wondered if he'd end up outing them right then and there. He never did of course, but he'd enjoyed the perverse game once he understood the rules. And part of the rules was that none of the men and women who fawned over him or called him brilliant or gushed about his books were his friends. Money, fame by association, connections – those were the things the people in his circle wanted...no, expected from him.

It would have helped if Luke had been like that, even just a little. At least then Gray could turn off that switch inside of himself that let him believe this time might be different. That maybe the things Luke needed from him had nothing to do with who he was but who he should have been before he'd allowed fame to grab hold of him and twist him into something he no longer recognized. But as far as he could tell, Luke didn't know the extent of his fame and more importantly, he hadn't even tried to find out. One Google search and Luke would have learned who he really was, how much he was worth and what the tabloids would have paid just to even know where Gray was hiding out. And if Luke knew the entire truth about why Gray was in Montana – well, he'd be set for life because Gray would pay any amount to keep his secret for as long as possible.

His ringing phone ripped Gray from his bout of self-pity and as much as he would have liked to ignore it, he'd been doing that for several weeks now and he knew he couldn't keep hiding his head in the sand. The ringtone told him exactly who it was so when he managed to pry the phone from his jacket pocket, he said, "Hey Sid."

Sidney Grant was a brilliant agent but Gray had no doubt that the guy would sell his own grandmother out for a lucrative contract or endorsement deal. "Gray, where the hell have you been? Do you have any idea of the shitstorm going on?"

"I'm fine, Sid, thanks for asking. How are you?"

"Cavelli is threatening the studio with a lawsuit and they're talking about pulling the plug on the whole deal!" Sid shouted. "And Foster is considering delaying your next book."

Gray took a deep breath and rolled onto his side. The act of holding the phone to his ear felt like too much and he wished now that he hadn't answered it. Sid hadn't even stopped long enough to let him answer and Gray let his eyes slide shut as the shrill voice began rattling off how much money Gray was losing, which translated to Sid losing money.

"Where are you? I'll come to you. We'll talk strategy."

"Sid," Gray said wearily. "What part of 'I need some time to myself' didn't you understand?"

Sid snorted and then rambled on like he hadn't spoken. Gray knew the one sided conversation could go on all night so he forced himself to an upright position so he could focus. "Sid, shut the fuck up and hear what I'm saying, okay?"

Sid finally fell silent but Gray could sense the man was barely holding his tongue. "I don't give a shit what Cavelli says or does – he's not right for the part and I'm not fucking signing off on him. And you and I both know Len Fogle isn't going to pull the plug on the deal… his studio's got too much money invested."

"But Foster…"

"Is trying to find any excuse to renegotiate my contract. Aren't you the one who says any publicity is good publicity? Ask them to send you the numbers on pre-orders and then ask them again if they're going to delay the release."

"We still need to have a response ready to go if Cavelli goes public."

"He's absolutely going to go public when the studio tells him he's not getting the part. And my response will be the same thing I told him when he threatened me…fuck off." Gray pinched the bridge of his nose as his head began to spin. "Good night, Sid," was all he said as he hung up the phone and tossed it on his nightstand. He was caught off guard at the sting of tears as another wave of nausea went through him and he climbed unsteadily to his feet. His last thought before he leaned over the toilet was the same one he'd had over and over in the motel room – he wished Luke was there to hold him.

CHAPTER 5

*L*uke watched Gray pick at his food but instead of saying something like he wanted to, Luke stood and took his own empty plate to the sink and rinsed it before putting it in the dishwasher. Gray had been home for two days and looked even worse now than he had then, though Luke wasn't sure how that was possible. But while Gray's physical appearance had started to change drastically, their interactions with each other had been exactly like they'd been before Gray left to go to Missoula for his mysterious hook up. The only exception had been their brief argument the day after Gray's return when Gray had seen the dishwasher. He'd offered his thanks but then he'd done something unexpected that had torn Luke up inside…he'd fucking paid Luke for installing the dishwasher. And just like that, their relationship had changed completely and while Luke hadn't touched the money Gray had left sitting on the counter for him, Gray hadn't taken it back either. If Luke had been smart, he would have taken the money and used it to get his ass back on the road. But he didn't want Gray's fucking money…he didn't know what the hell he wanted but he knew it wasn't that.

Luke reached for the bread on top of the fridge and tossed a couple of slices into the toaster. Once the bread was lightly browned, he put it on a plate and then went to the table and replaced the chicken and vegetables Gray had been pretending to eat with the toast. Luke put the uneaten food in the garbage and then returned to sit at the table. Gray hadn't touched the bread and a glance at his glass of water showed he hadn't had any of it either.

"You need to see a doctor, Gray," Luke finally said when he took in Gray's sunken eyes and pale skin. He looked like death warmed over. At the slight shiver that went through Gray's body, Luke got up and grabbed the throw from the back of the couch in the living room and dropped it carefully over his shoulders. Luke had already turned the thermostat up in the cabin and he'd even started a fire in the fireplace but Gray still seemed chilled. "It doesn't make sense that you'd get the stomach flu again so soon but in any case, you're too dehydrated. A doctor can give you fluids…"

Gray's dull eyes continued to stare out the window as he wrapped the throw around his body. It was like the man hadn't even heard him.

"Gray," Luke whispered as he put his hand over the hand Gray had resting on the table.

"What?" Gray asked in confusion as he finally turned his head to look at Luke. So Gray hadn't been hearing him. "Sorry," he mumbled as he finally noticed the toast in front of him. A small sigh went through him as he eyed the food and then he pulled his hand free of Luke's and ran it through his hair.

Luke was about to repeat his statement about Gray needing to see a doctor when he saw Gray pull his hand away from his head. Shock tore through Luke when he saw what Gray was holding in his hand and a silent scream of denial went through Luke's brain as he registered what he was seeing.

Gray stared at his own hand and then let out a little laugh. He turned his hand over and let the small chunk of hair fall onto the table next to his plate and Luke couldn't take his eyes off of it as everything clicked into place.

"Gray," was all he could manage to get out and Gray turned his suddenly too bright eyes back on him.

"Excuse me," Gray whispered and then he was climbing unsteadily

54

to his feet. It took Luke several long seconds to make his own body react and then he was up and following Gray to his bedroom. He found Gray standing in front of the mirror in his bathroom, his fingers stroking over his hair. When another, smaller clump pulled free, Gray just stared at himself in the mirror for a while. And then his knees started to buckle and Luke barely managed to reach him before he hit the ground. Gray's weight threw Luke off balance but he was able to maneuver them so that they were both on their knees, Gray's back pressed to his front. The blanket that had been draped around Gray's shoulders was bunched between them and Luke loosened his hold on Gray's chest long enough to pull the blanket free and get it settled back around Gray.

He heard another dry chuckle escape Gray's lips. "It's true," Gray said hoarsely. "None of it's really real until this," he whispered as he opened his palm to look at the lock of hair.

Luke felt tears burn his eyes as he leaned his head down so that his forehead was resting against the back of Gray's neck. "Why didn't you tell me?"

Gray just shook his head and his whole body began to shake. Luke felt moisture hit his forearm where it was wrapped around Gray's chest. He didn't need to look to know that the man in his arms was crying because a harsh sob tore from Gray's lips a moment later.

"It's okay, Gray, I've got you," Luke whispered against the back of Gray's neck as he wrapped his other arm around Gray and held him as tightly as he could.

~

"What kind is it?" Luke asked as he tightened his arm around Gray's back. If Gray thought it was strange that Luke was still holding him so closely as they were sitting on the bathroom floor with their backs against the bathtub, he didn't say anything or pull away. And Luke hadn't given it much thought other than that he wasn't ready to let go of Gray yet even though his heart wrenching sobs had finally eased.

"Testicular," Gray said quietly.

"That's...that's highly curable, right?"

Gray was quiet for so long that Luke felt heat flood his entire body even though they were sitting on the cold tile floor.

"It's spread to my liver."

Luke felt like he was going to be sick. Cancer. Gray had fucking cancer.

"My doctor is hoping the chemo will get rid of the tumors."

Tumors? Plural?

"So that's why you went to Missoula this week? For chemo?"

Gray nodded. "That was my second round. The first was on the day we met."

An unreasonable anger went through Luke. "God, Gray, did you stay at that motel just so I wouldn't know you were sick again?"

Gray stiffened against him and tried to pull away but Luke refused to release him. Luke took several deep breaths to try to stem his anger and then said, "Don't hospitals require someone to be with you when you're undergoing chemo?"

"I convinced the staff I had someone waiting for me."

"What about your friends? Your family?"

Gray just shook his head.

"No one knows?"

Gray struggled free from his grip and climbed to his feet. Luke stood and tried to grab Gray's arm to steady him but Gray shook him off and leaned against the sink. Gray stared at himself in the mirror for another long moment before he yanked open a drawer. He pulled out a black box of some kind and Luke flinched when he saw what was inside. It took several seconds for Gray to work the clippers free of the foam housing they were encased in and then he was plugging the cord into the outlet. The sound of the clippers was harsh.

"Gray," Luke said softly as he reached for the clippers.

But Gray sucked in a quick breath and then ran the clippers right down the middle of his head. His shorn hair fell away silently and Gray stopped to stare at the result. Tears began to flow down his cheeks as he tried to shave another strip of hair away but he was too overcome to hold the clippers without shaking so Luke took them away and unplugged them. He lowered his mouth to Gray's ear and whispered, "Let me do it, okay?"

Gray managed a nod and allowed Luke to lead him from the bathroom. He got Gray settled in a kitchen chair and found a nearby outlet. Gray flinched as soon as he turned the clippers on but he never once took his eyes off the grove of trees that he was staring at through the window. Luke draped a dish towel over Gray's shoulders and made quick work of shaving the rest of Gray's head before brushing the stray clumps of hair to the floor. He sat down in the chair next to Gray who finally turned to look at him.

"How does it look?"

Luke couldn't stop himself from reaching out to run his hand over the small amount of stubble that remained. He wanted to tell Gray he still looked just as hot but figured that might just be too much for Gray to deal with right now so he settled for "really good" instead.

Gray lifted his hand to run his fingers over his head and hesitated the instant he felt his scalp.

"You'll get used to it," Luke said. "And think about how much money you'll save on that expensive shampoo of yours," he added.

A smile flitted across Gray's lips and Luke felt a spark of hope for the first time since he'd watched Gray's hair appear between his fingers.

"I'm really tired," Gray murmured. "I'm going to go lie down for a bit."

"Can you try to drink some more water?" Luke asked. "You're really dehydrated, Gray. It's part of the reason you're feeling so run down."

Gray looked at the water and then shook his head. "Can't," he whispered. "The metal..."

"I can take you to the hospital...they can give you IV fluids-"

"No," Gray said sharply. "No hospitals. Can't risk being recognized," he murmured before he seemed to realize what he'd said. "I'm fine," he insisted stubbornly as he stood.

Luke followed him back to the bedroom and wasn't surprised

when Gray went to look at himself in the mirror. His expression remained blank as he studied his reflection and then he was pushing himself away from the sink and stumbling towards his bed. Luke steadied him as he pulled back the covers and within seconds of Gray's head hitting the pillow, he was out.

Luke dropped down to sit on the edge of the bed and studied Gray's features. He couldn't stop himself from reaching out to run his hand over Gray's drawn face. Helplessness went through him as he placed his fingers against Gray's throat. The too fast beat had Luke reaching for Gray's phone.

~

The cool air was welcoming against Luke's skin as he entered the small building. He was glad to see the waiting room was empty but the electronic doorbell that had announced his presence once he'd opened the door must have been heard in the back because he heard someone shout that they'd be right there. An old cat was sitting on top of the reception counter and as it meowed at him expectantly, Luke went over and began petting it. The cat's soft fur and purring helped ease some of the anxiety he was having about not being armed. His gun was under the front seat of Gray's truck and even though he felt naked without it, he knew the vet's police officer boyfriend wouldn't have missed Luke being armed since it was too hot out to be wearing any kind of jacket that would have concealed the weapon.

Footsteps grew closer and the cat quickly ditched him to run down to the opposite end of the counter. The man who appeared instantly began stroking the cat. "Hi, can I help you?" he asked, his wide smile bright and welcoming. Luke guessed the man to be in his late thirties with an average build and brown hair with just a hint of silver in it.

"Are you Dr. Winters?"

"I am," the man said as he picked up the cat and snuggled her against his chest. "Call me Dane."

"I don't have an appointment or anything," Luke said awkwardly. "I got your name from Gray's phone and Googled your address."

The man went on alert at the mention of Gray's name and then his eyes narrowed slightly, probably because he was wondering what the hell Luke was doing going through Gray's phone. "Is Gray okay?"

Luke didn't miss the suspicion in the man's voice or the way the cat pulled free of his hold and jumped back on the counter to seek out Luke's hand.

"Are you Luke?" Dane suddenly asked before Luke could get his next words out. Luke nodded and Dane seemed to visibly relax though Luke had no idea why. "Jax said you were staying with Gray. Everything okay?"

Luke had been rehearsing how to make his request since he'd left the cabin and it was only his eagerness to get back to make sure Gray was okay that had him saying, "He's not feeling well and has gotten pretty dehydrated. You carry saline, right?"

Any tension that had eased from Dane's frame came back in an instant. "You want to administer Gray an IV?"

The man's disbelief had Luke cringing. It did sound completely ridiculous. "I did some research and it looks like normal saline is the same formulation for animals as it is for humans - .9% sodium chloride."

"Are you a doctor?"

Luke shook his head. "I had some combat medic training."

Dane studied him for a long time before saying, "It's more than just the flu, isn't it?"

"What?"

"I saw Gray last week when he came to pick up Ripley. He said he was getting over the flu."

Luke wasn't sure how much to say. "It's more than just the flu," he confirmed. "Look, I know this is a lot to ask and believe me, if it wasn't necessary, I wouldn't be here. He's not critical yet but he will be soon if he doesn't get some fluids in him."

"I could lose my license if I do this," Dane said softly.

"I know," Luke admitted. He'd known that before he'd looked up

Dane's name in Gray's phone but that hadn't stopped him – hell, it had barely slowed him down. "Gray refuses to go to a hospital. If I need to, I'll go over his head and call 911…I just want to do everything I can before it gets to that point."

Dane nodded his head. "Makes sense that he doesn't want to go to the hospital," Dane said. "I'm sure the press would love to track him down to get his side of the story. Come with me."

"What story?" Luke couldn't help but ask as he followed Dane towards the back of the building.

"There's a rumor going around that Gray was having an affair with the actor who's going to be starring in the movies based on his books. The guy's supposedly straight and engaged to his very pregnant girl-friend so the press is having a field day."

Gray's reluctance to go to the ER had much greater meaning now. But Luke knew for a fact that it wasn't a scandalous relationship Gray was trying to hide.

Dane led him into a small room full of medical supplies and grabbed an empty box from underneath the counter which he gave to Luke to hold so he could start loading it up.

"What are his symptoms?" Dane asked as he worked.

"Dry skin, sunken eyes, he's easily confused. Chapped lips, rapid pulse."

Dane nodded. "And you've done this before?"

"Yeah. My unit didn't always have a medic on hand so things kind of fell to me."

Dane's eyes flipped up to his. "I want you to text me every hour until he's out of the woods and if there's no improvement by" – Dane glanced at his watch – "three, promise you'll take him to the ER and call me so I can meet you there." The man's tone left little room for argument. Not that Luke would have argued anyway – Dane clearly cared about Gray.

"How do you know him?" Luke asked Dane, though a part of him was nervous about learning the answer.

"I've been a fan of his books for a while but we met a couple of months ago at the bookstore in town."

"So you two weren't-"

"No," Dane said quickly, sparing Luke a brief glance. "Just friends...though maybe not even that," Dane said sadly.

"What do you mean?"

Dane shrugged. "Jax and I were having some problems then...well, I was having the problems and Jax was just trying to figure me out," he said with a self-deprecating chuckle.

"Did Gray come between you or something?"

"No...God, no," Dane said quickly. "Jax was the only one I wanted. Gray actually helped me figure that out. He told me to fight for what I wanted and never let go because life was too short for anything else."

A sick feeling went through Luke. God, had Gray known even then how sick he was? Had he been facing his disease by himself the whole time?

"Good advice, right?" Dane said softly and Luke realized the man had stopped loading the box and was staring at him thoughtfully. The words he wasn't saying rang loud and clear.

"Gray and I are just friends," Luke murmured.

Dane's eyes went from his to the box in his hand. "I'd buy that if I didn't see how scared you are for him," he said as he motioned to the box.

He supposed the easiest way to set Dane straight would be to tell him he wasn't interested in men but he couldn't force the words past his lips. He still wasn't interested in men...he was only interested in one man. The proof of that was standing right in front of him. Dane was a good looking guy, kind-hearted, sweet. And though Luke's encounter with Jax the other night had been brief, he hadn't missed how stunning the man was and that his build was similar to Gray's. But he didn't feel even a hint of attraction towards either man. Whatever was going on with him, it was unique to Gray and only Gray.

Luke was saved from having to come up with an adequate response when the bell went off indicating someone had entered the building. A loud voice called out, "Dane, you here?"

"Back here," Dane responded.

Luke saw Jax stiffen on seeing him when he entered the small supply room but he didn't hesitate to lean down and kiss Dane in greeting. "Where's Emma?" he asked as his hooded gaze glanced at Luke who'd automatically taken a few steps back to give the lovers some space.

"In the house with Mrs. Greene."

"Where's Gray?" was the next question out of Jax's mouth and Luke didn't miss the tension in the big man's frame as he looked at the supplies in the box.

"Tell you in a sec," Dane said softly and then his hand was stroking over Jax's arm as if to ease the man. And damn if it didn't just work because Jax immediately dropped his arms and laced his fingers through Dane's. The sight did something to Luke's insides that temporarily pushed away the stress of being in such close proximity to the lawman who was in full uniform and the knowledge that all the guy had to do was ask Luke for ID and he was screwed.

"Luke," Dane said gently and Luke finally tore his gaze from Jax's long enough to look at the vet. "I could come back to Gray's place with you and help out," he offered.

"Dane, I'm sorry..." Luke began to say but then shook his head. How could he tell the man that it would need to be Gray's decision if and how much he would say about his condition?

But Dane saved him by saying, "Remember to text me and ask him to call me when he's feeling better. And if you need anything, anything at all..."

Luke quickly nodded. "I'll call. And I'll make sure he calls you. Thank you," he added as he began backing towards the door. Jax's eyes narrowed again but he remained silent. Once Luke was out of sight, he hurried towards the front of the clinic. He heard lowered voices behind him but a quick glance over his shoulder showed that Jax wasn't following him. Still, he didn't manage a deep breath until he was actually in the truck and had pulled the gun from its hiding place and tucked it into his pants. Unfortunately, his relief was short-lived because after that, his only thought was to get to back Gray.

∾

*H*e finally felt warm, so it had to be a dream. Gray would have chuckled at the absurdity of it all if he'd been awake. He'd fallen pretty far to be so excited about something as simple as not feeling the endless, bone deep chill that had consumed him since the first time a nurse had stuck the needle in his arm that would deliver the poison that would have to slowly kill him in order to save him. What he wouldn't give for the good old days of dreaming about being buried balls deep in a hot guy with a tight ass. Hell, he'd even take the more standard - albeit fucked up - dream where he was standing on the sidelines of his own life watching everything he'd worked for come to fruition and wishing he could somehow undo it all.

No, warm was good. He'd take warm. It was that thought that had him snuggling farther under the covers but then he felt the tell-tale sting of the needle in his arm and he sat upright.

"No," he whispered as his gaze focused on the needle buried deep in his vein.

"Gray-"

"Not enough time," he muttered as he reached to yank the offending thing out of his body. He was finally feeling almost human.

"Gray, don't," he heard a stern voice order and then his hands were being gripped in a strong hold.

"Luke," he said as the final fog of sleep lifted. "I'm supposed to have a week in between treatments," he said desperately.

"It's just fluids, Gray," Luke said as he settled his weight onto the bed next to Gray.

Gray glanced up at the IV dangling from an eyelet attached to the wall. It was then that he realized he wasn't even in the hospital. He looked back down at the needle in his forearm. "What...who did this?"

"I did," Luke said quietly. "You were dangerously dehydrated. It was either this or the hospital."

The warmth that was spreading through Gray's body was nothing compared to the heat around his wrists and he glanced down to see that Luke was still holding his hands.

"Don't try to pull it out, okay?" Luke said and when Gray nodded, Luke released him. "How do you feel?"

"Good," Gray responded. And he did. Besides feeling warm, he didn't feel like he'd gone ten rounds with a heavyweight boxer and the endless nausea was actually non-existent for once. "How long have I been asleep?"

"Almost sixteen hours," Luke answered.

"How did you do this?" Gray asked as he motioned to the IV.

Luke's eyes shifted away from him for a moment before finally meeting his and holding him with an intense, almost heated look. "I asked Dane for the IV supplies."

All the warmth Gray was feeling disappeared and his throat closed up with despair. "No," he whispered.

Luke's hand came up to palm his cheek so that he had no choice but to look at Luke. "Gray, I had no choice."

"I didn't want him to know...I didn't want any of them to know."

"I just told Dane you were sick – I didn't give him details. But he's a smart guy..."

The rough skin against Gray's cheek felt good and Gray wished like hell he could lean into it, even if just for a moment. Or better yet, wrap his arms around Luke's neck and bury his face against the man's strong body where nothing could touch him anymore.

"Gray, I had no choice," Luke whispered again and it was the desperate tone that had Gray forcing himself to nod.

"I'm sorry, it's okay," he finally said and he realized it was true. "I trust Dane – he won't say anything."

"He said the press were trying to find you to ask you about some story."

Shit, that was something Gray had absolutely no interest in discussing with Luke because then he'd have to admit to a mess of crap he was trying to forget. And luckily, his body was cooperating with him and he didn't have to lie when he said, "Luke, I've really got to take a piss."

Luke chuckled and the sound washed over Gray's whole body like a caress. Luke glanced up at the nearly empty IV bag and said, "Okay, let me take this out." His expert fingers made quick work of removing the needle from his arm and covering the area with a Band-Aid. Gray quickly climbed to his feet and was grateful for the hand that wrapped around his elbow to steady him until he got his bearings.

"Take it slow," Luke murmured.

"Really not going to be able to do that," Gray gritted out which earned him another laugh from Luke. God, the guy's voice, touch and that fucking laugh were turning him inside out.

Luke helped him to the bathroom but blessedly didn't follow him inside. When he was done, Luke was waiting for him. "You up to trying to eat something?"

The thought of food instantly brought back the dreaded metallic taste but it wasn't as strong as it had been the day before so he nodded. He managed to make it to the kitchen on his own two feet but stopped when he took in the sight of the doorless cabinets. "Wow," he said.

"Yeah, that," Luke mumbled. "Been trying to keep busy," was all he said. "Sit," he ordered gently and Gray turned to go to the table. As soon as he sat, things started appearing in front of him. Various glasses and bottles full of liquid, a banana, a peach, some crackers and what looked like a container of pudding.

"So I did some research while you were sleeping and I think there's a couple things we can try that might not taste as bad to you," Luke began. "Instead of plain water, you can add some citrus flavor – the acid will help balance out the metallic taste." Luke pushed a couple of glasses forward.

Caught off guard, Gray could only stare at the first glass.

"Gray..."

The way Luke whispered his name had a knot of something drawing tight deep inside of Gray's gut but he managed to take a sip of the first glass. The awful taste was there but it wasn't as pronounced. He tried the others. The last one actually tasted decent and he ended up taking several long swallows that had Luke smiling widely.

"Good?" Luke asked excitedly.

Gray was so overwhelmed by how light the man's expression looked that he could only nod.

"So for food, they say soft, mild tasting fruits are good..."

Gray only heard half of what Luke was saying because it was finally hitting him what this man had done for him. Not only had he taken the time to research the foods and drinks that would be easier on Gray's body, he'd also gone to Dane looking for the help that Gray had no idea he'd even needed. The implications were stunning. Luke hadn't just risked his own safety by leaving the cabin, he'd gone to the home of a police officer who could have easily detained him and discovered who he was.

"Why did you do this?" Gray heard himself ask.

At the interruption, Luke looked at him like it was a ridiculous question. "Because you needed it."

Gray couldn't manage to say anything after that and it was all he could do not to lean in and brush his lips over Luke's so he forced himself to start trying the different foods Luke had laid out. Most of them didn't taste like metal but they didn't taste like anything else either because all Gray could focus on was Luke's soul shattering statement.

Because you needed it.

CHAPTER 6

"I didn't even know this was here," Gray murmured.

"You never explored the property?" Luke asked as he double-checked to make sure the blanket was still covering Gray as much as possible. Although the temperature was well above freezing, he knew Gray's body couldn't afford to lose too much body heat. He checked his watch so he'd be able to keep track of the time.

"No."

"How come?"

"Too preoccupied I guess."

"You knew you were sick when you came out here?" Luke ventured.

Gray nodded. "I got the diagnosis a couple of months ago. I'd felt something one morning in the shower but I kept putting off a visit to my doctor." Gray's laugh sounded ugly. "I was such a fool...I actually thought nothing could touch me. I thought I'd climbed so high that nothing could take me down. And then the doctor throws out the C word and the first thing I did was call him a quack. Then he tells me he needs to cut both my balls off. I told him to fuck off and then I went looking for a real doctor. Only the second one told me the same exact thing. I thought for sure the third one would be the charm."

Gray fell silent as he shifted on the log. Ripley was uncharacteristically solemn and lay at Gray's feet instead of playing in the creek like she usually did. "We should go inside," Luke said softly.

"Just a few more minutes," Gray whispered, his eyes settled on some far off point in the darkness.

"Did you have the surgery?"

A nod and then Gray's eyes dropped to the ground. "Neutered just like a dog," he croaked.

"Gray-"

"I was paranoid that the news would get out so I came out here for radiation treatments. I'd bought this place sight unseen a few years ago as a place I could come to get some writing done. My lawyer set it up so I could buy it using a land trust – that way it wouldn't be as easy for people to find out it was mine. And I figured Dare was small enough that the chances anyone would recognize me were slim to none."

"Why all the secrecy?"

"My career really took off a couple years ago when my book hit the bestseller list. I wasn't a household name or anything but then Hollywood started knocking on my door. After that, everything just snowballed. I signed a contract for my first three books in the series to be made into movies – the deal was worth millions and suddenly I went from being a nobody who spent fifteen hours a day in front of his computer to a guy rubbing elbows with celebrities on the red carpet. Talk shows, magazine articles…it was surreal. It was my dream come true."

Gray drew the blanket tighter around his body but before Luke could insist they go inside, he continued. "I took advantage of it – all of it. I had stylists telling me how to dress, publicists who told me what to say and how to say it so I could sell my brand. A personal trainer, chef, you name it. And everybody and their brother wanted to be my friend. But the best part was the men - it was like God had handed me a fucking buffet.

"I loved it, you know? The attention. Guys who wouldn't have given me the time of day before all of a sudden wanted me. But I knew it wasn't me that they wanted, not really. Didn't stop me from taking what they were offering, though."

Hearing about Gray's active sexual history caused jealousy to burn through every cell in Luke's body but he managed to keep his agitation to himself and was actually proud when his voice sounded steady as he said, "It doesn't make you a bad person, Gray."

"What does it make me?" Gray asked. "I didn't give a shit that the men I was with were married or closeted or believed that we would have some kind of relationship going forward. I used them."

"So what, you think this is the universe's way of punishing you?"

Gray dashed at his eyes. "It's what I thought at first. I didn't have any other explanation for what was happening and I needed a fucking reason," Gray said vehemently. "But when the doctor told me the cancer had spread…" Gray shook his head slowly.

"That's when your doctor said you needed chemo?"

Gray nodded. "The radiation hadn't been that bad so I figured the chemo wouldn't be either."

"Didn't they tell you what to expect?"

"Yeah, they did. I just chose to believe I was going to be the exception. People have been telling me my whole life that I wasn't going to be anything…to accept my limitations and settle. I figured cancer would just be one more thing I had to say 'Fuck off' to. The nausea, the hair," - Gray ran his hand over his scalp – "none of it was going to apply to me."

"Why didn't you tell anyone?"

"Who?" Gray said with another one of his harsh laughs. "My parents who hate me almost as much as they hate each other? The half-brother I'm not on speaking terms with? My so called management team?"

"Friends then?" Luke said. "Dane, Jax."

"Jax hates my guts and Dane…Dane's had enough of his own shit to deal with. He's finally in a good place."

"Dane was really worried about you, Gray. And the fact that he gave me the supplies I needed…he risked a lot by doing that. That cop

– Jax – he could have stopped me at any point to look at my ID or ask me questions but he didn't."

Gray didn't answer him but Luke could tell he was mulling over Luke's words. "How come you don't want people to know what you're going through?"

"In the beginning I didn't want to deal with the stigma of it, you know? I mean, testicular cancer – the treatment is pretty obvious. Sure, a lot of people would have been supportive but they would have looked at me differently – like I was half a man. And I didn't want to deal with the questions. But then when I found out it was in my liver, I was terrified that the public would expect me to be some kind of role model or something."

"Why does that scare you?" Luke asked.

"People need their role models to be strong and accepting and know all the right things to say. I'm scared shitless and all I want to do is yell at the top of my lungs that I don't want to die."

When Gray's voice cracked, Luke put his arm around his shoulders and pulled him to his chest. There were no harsh sobs this time but Luke could feel moisture seeping through his shirt where Gray's head was pressed up against his heart and Gray's fingers were biting into his sides.

Luke wished he could find the right words to say, but everything that entered his mind seemed trite and as much as he wanted to tell Gray he'd be okay, it was a promise he just couldn't make. So instead, he just placed his free hand over the back of Gray's neck and held him so that the other man would know that he wasn't alone anymore.

~

Gray swallowed hard just before knocking on the door. He wasn't surprised when it opened within seconds since he'd asked Dane if it was okay if he came over. But it wasn't Dane who answered.

Jax was holding Emma in his arms but anything he might have been about to say died a quick death and he just stared at Gray in horror. It sucked to have to stand there as Jax tried to register what he was seeing but Gray knew it was a lot to take in – there were times when he no longer recognized himself in the mirror. While the cotton cap he'd bought from the specialized cancer shop at the hospital earlier in the week covered most of his head, there was no way to hide his missing eyebrows. Add in his pale skin and weight loss and he knew he was barely recognizable.

"Gray," Jax managed to whisper and then he was stepping back to let Gray enter.

"Hey," Gray said as he stepped inside. "Thanks for letting me come over so early."

"Yeah…it's no problem," Jax said and Gray would have enjoyed how flustered the man was if he hadn't seen the dreaded pity in his eyes too. Luckily, Emma chose that moment to extend her arms towards him.

"Can I?" Gray asked.

"Of course," Jax quickly said and handed the baby over. Emma wriggled in his arms as her chubby hands began patting his face and Gray couldn't help but smile. She reached up and began playing with the cap and Gray figured it was as good a time as any to bite the bullet so he pulled the cap off his head and handed it to her.

The sound of something breaking had Gray jerking his gaze to the right. In the doorway leading to the kitchen stood Dane with a very unbalanced tray in his hands. There were two cups still on it as well as what Gray could only assume were containers for sugar and cream. A third cup lay in pieces at Dane's feet. Gray was about to say something when Jax darted to Dane's side and rescued the tray before the rest of the contents hit the floor.

"Gray," Dane whispered just before he put his hand over his mouth. Then he was surging forward and dragging Gray into his arms.

"I'm okay, Dane," he whispered against Dane's ear as he heard a strangled cry leave Dane's lips. Luke had been right – how had Gray not seen that these men cared about him?

Dane nodded against him and then said, "Why don't you take

Emma into the living room? I'm just going to help Jax clean up," Dane managed to get out. Gray suspected the man also needed a moment to get himself together because Dane quickly turned away from him and wiped at his face.

Gray carried Emma into the living room and sat in one of the arm chairs and balanced the little girl on his lap. He used the cap to play peek a boo with her and couldn't help but smile when she giggled every time he did it. Several minutes passed before her fathers joined them. Jax was carrying the tray and Dane was right behind him with the coffee pot. Neither man made a move to take the baby from him as they settled down on the couch. The sight of Jax lacing his fingers through Dane's left such a longing in Gray's soul that he actually had to tear his eyes away. How many times had he been sitting next to Luke in the last week and wished he could touch him like that? Whether they were watching TV or sitting on their log by the creek, Gray always found himself wanting just a little more than just the quiet strength that Luke exuded.

"So yeah, I have cancer," Gray finally said since neither man seemed capable of speech. "God, that's the first time I've said that out loud," he said softly as he bounced Emma on his knee.

Dane managed to recover first. "How long?"

"I was diagnosed a couple of months ago. Testicular cancer," he added. "It's spread but my doctors are hopeful that chemo will do the trick."

"What can we do, Gray?" Jax asked. The question came as a surprise since he'd expected to get the third degree about not telling them sooner.

"I'm good right now, but I'll let you know." He shifted his gaze to Dane. "Thank you for what you did. Luke told me what you risked...I didn't even realize how bad it had gotten."

"I'm glad he was there," Dane said. "Dehydration can get really bad, really fast."

Gray nodded. He had no doubt that Luke had likely saved his life because he'd been too out of it to realize the danger he'd been in.

"Do you need any more saline?" Dane asked.

"No, I don't think so. I had a treatment a couple of days ago and the fluids helped me get back on my feet pretty quickly. Luke also found some foods and drinks that I can tolerate. I have one more treatment next week and I think he said you gave him enough to get me through that."

"Do you need a ride to your treatment?" Jax asked.

Gray shook his head. "Luke is taking me." It was something he and Luke had argued about especially since Luke had insisted on accompanying him into the hospital for the actual treatment. Even with the private room and limited staff treating him, Gray had still been on edge the entire time that someone would recognize Luke. Not that there'd be any reason that they would since Gray had been monitoring the headlines and hadn't seen any stories about a man fitting Luke's description. He'd been tempted on more than one occasion to do an Internet search on Luke's name and Fort Benning where Luke was stationed to see what came up but it had been a line he just didn't want to cross. He trusted Luke and wanted the man to trust him.

Gray shifted his eyes to Jax and said, "I owe you an apology."

Jax was caught off guard by the statement.

"I never meant to come between you and Dane," he said softly.

"Gray-" Dane began to say but he saw Jax tighten his hold on Dane's hand and Dane fell silent.

"We're good, Gray. Jealousy wasn't a great color on me."

He knew Jax was letting him off easy considering how he'd goaded the man on more than one occasion so he just nodded.

"So Luke is still staying with you?" Jax ventured, his unasked question clear as day.

"Just till he gets back on his feet. He's kind of starting over," Gray hedged. It was as close to the truth as he was going to be able to get. "We're not...we're not what I made you believe we were a couple of weeks ago. We're just friends."

He saw Dane and Jax look at each other briefly. "Gray, what I saw the other day when he came here wasn't just about friendship," Dane said.

Gray's heart seized up but he quickly dismissed the wayward emotion. "He's straight, Dane. He's just a really good guy, that's all."

Dane looked like he wanted to say something else but Gray didn't have the emotional strength to deal with arguing over something that just wasn't going to happen. Even if by some miracle Luke's interest in him did straddle the line between friendship and something else, what the hell did Gray have to offer? He was a shell of a man with an uncertain future. And that didn't even factor in the reality of Luke's situation.

"I should probably head out," Gray said as he climbed to his feet and handed Emma to Jax. Between the offers to drive him back to his place and the promises he had to make to keep them posted on his condition and call if he needed anything, it took Gray a good ten minutes to get on the road back to his place. While the visit had gone better than he'd expected, he still found himself wishing Luke had been at his side. His growing attraction to the man was becoming problematic but it was his heart that was really starting to take a beating because what it was feeling went beyond friendship or gratitude.

In the three weeks since they'd met, Gray hadn't learned as much as he would have liked about the quiet man who'd become such a fixture in his life. But the things he did know were all things that tugged at something deep inside of him. Like how smart Luke was even though he didn't seem to think so himself. Or how invested he got in things, whether it was the sci-fi movies he loved so much or the various projects he'd been working on around the cabin or the attention he gave Ripley. He was a stickler for details but also had no problem laughing at himself if something didn't turn out the way he'd planned. But one of Gray's favorite things to watch over the last few weeks was how relaxed Luke had become. He no longer carried his gun around on his person all the time and didn't seem to be constantly scanning his surroundings like he had in the early days. There'd even been a couple of nights where Luke had actually fallen asleep on the couch while they were watching TV and Gray had been able to just sit and enjoy how at peace he looked.

But Gray wasn't foolish enough to believe that whatever was happening would become his new normal, whatever the outcome might be in a couple weeks when his doctor would run the tests that would show if the chemo had done its job. At some point Gray would have to return to his obligations and Luke…well, he had no idea what Luke was going to do. It physically pained him to know how much trouble Luke was in. He'd only ever admitted to someone framing him for murder but it was clear Luke felt he had no one to turn to for help. Gray had approached the subject a few days earlier with another offer to help him get the best lawyer money could buy but Luke had casually brushed off the conversation with an excuse that he needed to finish up something in the shed. It had been frustrating to not give back to the man who'd given him so much.

The subject of his thoughts was just walking around the side of the cabin when Gray pulled into the driveway. Luke had offered to go with him to Dane and Jax's but Gray had been too worried that Luke and Jax would have a run-in that would put Luke at risk, so he'd made the excuse that it was something he needed to do on his own. It was complete crap of course, but also a good decision because Gray knew he was becoming too reliant on Luke's quiet strength.

"How did it go?" Luke asked as Gray got out of the car.

"About as well as can be expected, I guess," Gray said as he tried to ignore the need to reach out and touch Luke. It would be so easy because Luke was only a half a foot away.

"I wish you'd let me come with you," Luke said softly and to Gray's surprise, he stepped closer and put his arm up on the side of the truck, essentially caging Gray in. Even though they were about the same size, Gray still felt slight as Luke's big body brushed his briefly.

Despite the sudden dryness in his mouth, Gray managed to change the subject. "How's the kitchen coming?" Luke didn't answer him right away and a shudder went through Gray when Luke's gaze dropped to his mouth. Dear God, was the man actually…

Ripley's excited barking ripped Gray from his thoughts and he felt Luke tense up and then quickly step away from him. Luke's hand reached behind his back and Gray knew he was instinctively looking for his gun – unfortunately, Gray had no idea if this was one of the times Luke had chosen to go without it.

A black Mercedes was pulling into the driveway behind Gray's truck and Gray sucked in a sharp breath when he recognized the driver. Luke's hand was still at his back so Gray quickly reached out and grabbed his arm. "It's okay," he said. "It's my brother."

Luke flashed him a quick look of surprise. "I thought you guys didn't talk."

"We don't," Gray responded as an overwhelming sense of dread took hold of him.

"You didn't want your family to know," Luke observed.

Gray shook his head.

"Go inside," Luke said. "I'll tell him to go."

Luke was already moving forward when Gray grabbed his wrist. "No," he murmured. "I'd like to see him." The truthful statement surprised even himself.

Gray closed the truck's door and watched as his brother climbed out of what Gray could only assume was a rental since it had Montana plates. His brother hadn't changed much since Gray had last seen him almost three years ago. His dark hair was short on the sides and just a little longer on top. A pair of dark sunglasses hid his blue eyes and he had a little bit of a five o'clock shadow going on. Even though he was nearly seven years younger than Gray, he was almost an inch taller and had a muscular build that his custom-made suit complemented.

As he approached, Gray saw the moment his brother noticed Gray's appearance and while his sunglasses hid his reaction, his step faltered and his lips parted just a little bit.

"Roman," Gray said quietly as he extended his hand.

Roman recovered quickly and shook his hand and then peeled his sunglasses off. Whatever surprise might have been in his gaze had been carefully schooled into a blank expression. It was something Roman was an expert at.

"Gray," Roman said in acknowledgement before shifting his gaze to Luke.

"Luke, this is my brother, Roman Blackwell. Roman, this is Luke."

"Half-brother," Roman corrected as he shook Luke's hand. Gray sighed at Roman's words – no matter how many times he referred to Roman as his brother, Roman always pointed out that they weren't quite real brothers.

"Why don't you guys head inside to talk?" Luke suggested as the breeze kicked up. "I'm going to finish some stuff up in the shed," he added. Luke didn't move until Gray nodded in agreement.

Gray remained silent as he led Roman into the cabin since he didn't have a clue as to what to say to the man who'd only ever resented him. Not that Roman didn't have reason to, Gray supposed, now that he had the luxury of hindsight.

"Coffee?" Gray asked once they reached the kitchen. It looked surprisingly clean even if the cabinets were all still missing but it looked like Luke was making good progress.

"Yes, please," Roman said stiffly.

It took just a few minutes to get the coffee going and while he waited for it to brew, he got a mug out and put it on the table in front of the chair Roman had sat down in. "Black, right?" Gray asked.

Roman seemed surprised by the comment but just nodded.

Gray got himself some of the lemon-lime flavored water that proved to be the easiest on his palate and then carried the coffee pot to the table and set it down in front of Roman.

"You're not having any?" Roman asked as he poured himself a cup while Gray settled into the chair across from him.

Gray shook his head.

"Never thought I'd see the day when you turned down a cup of coffee," Roman murmured as he put the pot back down.

"Yeah, well, it doesn't exactly agree with me anymore," Gray said as he pulled his cap off. Roman's hard gaze flashed with something as his eyes shifted to Gray's bald head. There was a brief moment where some undeterminable emotion lingered in Roman's expression but it didn't last long.

"You're sick," was all Roman said.

Gray was too drained to go through all of this for a second time in less than an hour so he just said, "What are you doing here, Roman?"

77

"Victoria was worried about you."

Gray had been in the process of taking a drink of water and nearly choked when he heard his mother's name. It wasn't unusual to hear Roman refer to their mother by her first name since it was what she had told Roman to call her when he'd made the mistake of asking if he could call her "Mom" after their father had brought him home the day after Roman's mother's funeral. Gray hadn't known much about Roman when his father announced that he had a little brother. He'd managed to garner bits and pieces of information over the years but even that was limited. What he did know was that his half-brother had been the product of one of Gray's father's dalliances with one of many mistresses and that the boy's mother had killed herself when Roman was only ten. For some unknown reason, Gray's father had decided to take the boy in since he had no other family and Gray's mother either hadn't been given any say in the matter, or his father had found some means to gain his mother's acquiescence. Neither scenario had meant that Roman was a welcome addition to the family and at seventeen, Gray had had no interest in connecting with the little boy who'd initially followed him everywhere. By the time he'd matured enough to see how cruelly he'd treated Roman, his brother had checked out of any potential relationship they might have had.

"Mom asked you to come and check on me?" Gray managed to get out. Since he hadn't gotten even one phone call from his mother in the weeks since he'd left L.A., he found the idea unbelievable, but then again, what other reason would his brother have for searching him out?

Roman just shrugged and took a sip of his coffee. It struck Gray then how he and his parents had failed Roman. Not once but over and over again. The young boy who'd been thrust into their lives hadn't had any choice in the matter and instead of being welcomed by adults who should've helped him grieve the loss of his mother, he'd been ridiculed and openly disparaged.

"How did you find me?" Gray asked.

"Marina let it slip."

Marina, his realtor who'd boasted about her ability to maintain confidentiality for her many celebrity clients. Since Roman was a property developer, it didn't surprise Gray to learn he and Marina knew each other.

"I wasn't aware she knew you and I were..."

He'd been about to say brothers but knew Roman would correct him which would only piss him off further so he settled for saying "related" instead.

Another annoying shrug but it was the way Roman dropped his eyes to his restless hands for a moment that had Gray saying, "She didn't know, did she? Jesus, Roman, did you fuck her just to find out where I was?"

Roman's chilly gaze lifted once more. "Marina was all too eager to dish about you after that shit with Cavelli went down. Fucking her was a perk."

Fanfuckingtastic.

"How long have you been sick?" Roman suddenly interjected.

"Couple months."

Roman didn't react in any way. He just asked, "Victoria and Walt don't know?"

Hearing his father referred to as Walt was just as strange as hearing Roman call his mother Victoria. And even though Roman and their father actually shared blood, Gray's mother had decreed that Roman wouldn't be calling his own father "Dad" anytime he was in her presence so he'd just resorted to calling him by his first name too.

"No," Gray said and he didn't bother to ask Roman not to tell them. Roman could and would do whatever the hell he wanted – he owed Gray nothing.

"Who's the guy?" Roman asked.

That was the ultimate question. Who was Luke?

"That answers that," Roman said softly and Gray looked up to see a slight smile folding up the edges of Roman's mouth. It was so strange to see his brother smile that it actually took Gray a second to realize what Roman was inferring.

"We're just friends," Gray said in irritation. He felt like a parrot because he'd been having this same conversation with Dane and Jax less than an hour earlier. Not to mention the many times he had to repeat the phrase over and over in his mind to try to remind himself that Luke was just a friend – a very straight friend.

Roman had the decency not to argue with him. They both fell into an awkward silence before Roman whispered, "Is it curable?"

Holy shit? Was his brother actually worried about him? The thought was so unexpected that it took Gray a second to answer and he saw his brother visibly stiffen and then open his mouth. Before Roman could blow off the question, Gray said, "My doctor is hopeful. I have one more round of chemo and then he'll do a CT to see if the tumors are gone or if it's spread any further."

Roman seemed to swallow hard and the move actually had a surge of hope going through Gray. What if it wasn't too late to salvage a relationship with his brother? What if he could make up for the poor excuse of a big brother he'd been?

"So you off to some exotic location to build cabanas and golf courses?" Gray asked.

Another small smile.

"Bermuda," Roman said.

Gray hadn't ever been to one of the many resorts his brother had built all around the world but he'd heard of them.

"Maybe I'll finally be able to afford a stay at one soon," Gray joked, although he wasn't far off since Roman's clientele were some of the wealthiest men and women in the world.

"Maybe," Roman said with a slight nod and when his eyes lifted to meet Gray's, it was all Gray could do not to get up and pull his brother into his arms for a hug.

"You think you might want to come back this way on your way home?" Gray asked as Roman rose to his feet.

Roman seemed surprised by the indirect invitation and Gray steeled himself for rejection. But instead, Roman said, "Might be a few weeks."

"I'll be here."

His brother studied him long and hard and then bobbed his head before turning and heading towards the door.

"Roman-"

Roman tensed but turned before he reached the door.

"Tell Mo-Victoria that I'm good. And thanks."

There was no acknowledgement on Roman's expression just before he turned and left the cabin but that was just fine with Gray. What Roman had just given him was more than Gray could have asked for.

Gray got up to watch his brother's car pull out of the driveway. The door opened a moment later when Luke entered and Gray instantly flashed to the moment Luke's big body had caged his against the truck.

"How did it go?" Luke asked as he carried one of the cabinet doors into the kitchen and put it on the counter.

"Really good," Gray managed to say even though his throat had dried up at the sight of Luke. Fuck, his attraction was getting out of control. He absolutely did not want to fuck up his budding friendship with this man. "My mom asked him to check on me."

Luke's brows lifted. "You going to call her? Put her mind at ease?"

Gray thought about it a moment and then reached into his pocket for his phone. "Yeah, yeah, I am."

"You want me to leave?" Luke asked.

Gray shook his head as he found his mother's phone number. He settled back down into the chair while it rang and then watched Luke holding the cabinet door up to check it against the base on the wall. It had been Luke's suggestion to strip and re-stain the cabinets to give them a more modern feel rather than buying brand new cabinets. As usual, Luke's instinct had been spot on because the cabinets still looked rustic but the new stain made them look fresh and clean.

"Looks good," Gray murmured and his heart flip-flopped when Luke cast him a smile over his shoulder. But the real distraction came when Luke leaned over to check something against the wall and a strip of skin was revealed where his shirt rode up just above his tight ass. The gun was tucked in his jeans but Gray barely noticed it because he was too busy ogling the man's flexing muscles. He also didn't notice his mother's annoyed voice until she said "hello" for the third time.

"Hey Mom, it's me," Gray said.

"Gray," his mother replied, the all too familiar thread of annoyance in her tone. "Sweetheart, now's not a good time. I'm about to meet with the van Horns to talk about a re-design of their house in the Hamptons." Her impatience made something deep inside Gray curl up and die.

"I...I was just calling to check in," Gray murmured.

"I do hope you've straightened out all that nonsense with that... that actor," she said with distaste. "I've had three clients ask me about you and your...proclivities."

Gray closed his eyes. "Sorry to have bothered you, Mom. Good luck with the van Horns," he said quietly and then hung up the phone.

"You okay?" he heard Luke ask and he opened his eyes to see Luke watching him intently.

"I'm nearly forty years old but I hear that tone in her voice and it puts me right back there, you know?"

"Back where?"

"Back to when I kept trying to figure out who they wanted me to be and kept coming up short."

A heavy hand came to rest on his and sparks of electricity shot up Gray's entire arm. He pulled his hand free of Luke's because he was just too vulnerable to try to rein in his need for the other man. "Roman said she was worried about me."

"You think he lied? Why would he do that?" Luke asked. "Do you think he wanted to hurt you?"

Gray thought back to the way his brother had looked at him just before he'd left. Like he'd wanted to say more. "No," Gray finally said. "I don't think so. I think he used her as an excuse."

"To check on you himself," Luke observed.

Gray smiled. "I think so. I didn't think he'd ever forgive me for how I treated him when he was a kid but maybe this is my chance to fix things."

"What happened between you two?"

"It's a long story," Gray warned.

Luke was quiet for a moment before saying, "I'm not going anywhere."

That statement and the way Luke's eyes seemed to burn right through him had Gray's body drawing up tight with desire. But instead of leaning across the table to drag Luke's mouth to his, Gray leaned back in his chair and started talking.

CHAPTER 7

*L*uke couldn't manage to sit still so he got up and started studying all the doctor's degrees and awards that hung in his office. Ivy league school, residency at a prestigious hospital – that had to be good, right? So what the hell was the guy doing in some community hospital in Montana?

"This guy, he's good, right?" he asked Gray who was sitting in one of the chairs across from the doctor's nearly pristine desk.

"He's good," Gray responded. His voice sounded dull. Not that Luke could blame the man considering whatever news he was about to get would change his life going forward.

They'd already been sitting in the doctor's office for nearly fifteen minutes and Luke was on the verge of hunting down the man himself and telling him to get his ass in here and tell them that everything was going to be okay – that the suffering Gray had gone through had paid off.

Gray's last chemotherapy treatment had been a week ago and he hadn't been able to bounce back as quickly from it as he had the week before. Although he'd stopped vomiting within twenty-four hours, the long term effect of the treatments had started to take their toll on him and he spent most of his time in bed or resting on the couch. The weight loss had continued and Luke was estimating that the man was a good thirty pounds underweight. But it was the mental strain that had concerned Luke the most because as the date when Gray would learn his fate had drawn closer and closer, Gray had become more quiet and withdrawn. And it wasn't like Luke could really pull Gray out of it because Luke was feeling the exact same way.

The helplessness had become almost crippling for Luke and it was a stark reminder of his childhood when he'd had no control over his future or any reason to hope for more than whatever each day would bring. All those things had changed when he'd turned eighteen and been given the freedom to make his own decisions. He'd been scared shitless then too but at least he'd had the benefit of being able to make his own choices. Now all he could do was watch the man who'd become frighteningly important to him endure the incessant torture of not knowing what his future held or if he even had one.

Luke's emotional attachment to Gray had only strengthened his physical need for the other man even though Gray barely resembled the man he'd met on the side of the road a month earlier. He'd gotten past the strangeness of being attracted to a man rather quickly, although the unknown did frighten him somewhat. The part he was struggling with the most was what would happen if he did pursue any kind of relationship with Gray. And that was assuming the experienced and self-proclaimed playboy would even be interested in starting something up with a guy who'd never so much as touched another man in a sexual way and could count on one hand how many women he'd been with.

While Luke had managed to put the threats in his life out of his mind for the past couple of weeks, he wasn't foolish enough to think he was out of danger. Even if by some miracle he could convince the cops of his innocence, it didn't mean that the man hunting him would suddenly stop. And it didn't mean that he wouldn't use any means necessary to get to Luke. Which meant that every day Luke stayed with Gray was another day he risked putting Gray in the crosshairs of a man who'd already proven he wouldn't let anything stand in the way of his rise to power.

"Luke, come sit. You're making me nervous," Gray said quietly.

Luke returned to his seat but didn't even notice he was tapping his foot incessantly until Gray reached over to put his hand on Luke's fist where it was resting on his thigh.

"It's going to be okay," Gray said as he gave Luke a reassuring squeeze. Before Gray could draw his hand away, Luke snagged it in his and then shifted in his seat so he was facing Gray. He couldn't stop himself from extending his free arm and cupping his hand around the back of Gray's neck and drawing him closer until their foreheads were touching.

"No matter what happens, I'm here," Luke said firmly, even though he had no idea how he could follow through with the promise.

"Don't make promises you can't keep," Gray whispered. Their mouths were so close that Luke could feel Gray's warm breath fanning over his lips. Gray's eyes had closed at some point but the way his hand was clenching Luke's told Luke everything he needed to know. Gray was scared to death.

"I'm here," Luke repeated, his tone almost harsh. God, it would be so easy to draw Gray's lips to his. He was actually doing it before he could stop himself but the door opening behind them had him releasing Gray instead.

"Sorry to keep you waiting, Gray," the doctor said as he closed the door behind him and went to his desk. Gray had released Luke's hand so Luke had no choice but to clench his fists again in an effort to gain enough control to keep himself from leaping across the desk and demanding that the doctor tell them what they wanted to hear...no, *needed* to hear.

～

*G*ray's hand was shaking violently as he pushed the down button for the elevator. He had no idea if Luke noticed or not because the man hadn't looked at him even once after they'd left the doctor's office. In fact, he hadn't said a word. Of course,

Gray hadn't fared any better. Even now, he was having trouble wrapping his head around it.

Remission.

It had taken several long seconds after the doctor had said the word for it to actually register in Gray's muddled brain. He'd spent so much time planning how to deal with the news that he'd need more treatment or surgery that he hadn't given much thought to what it would mean if the doctor said that word. At his lowest point when he'd been too tired to crawl out of bed, he'd asked Luke to bring him his laptop and he'd started researching charities that he'd leave the majority of his estate to. Never in his wildest dreams would he have thought it would be such a struggle to hear the one word he'd hoped and prayed he'd hear.

The elevator door slid open and he stepped inside and leaned back against the wall and put his hands on the rail to make sure he stayed upright since he couldn't trust his shaky legs to do the job. Luke's body brushed his briefly as he reached to press the button for right parking level. Luke was so quiet that a moment of panic went through Gray and he whispered, "You heard it too, right?"

Luke finally looked at him and the turbulent emotion in the man's stormy eyes caught Gray off guard. "He said I was in remission, right?" Gray managed to get out.

Luke nodded and then just stared at him for a pregnant moment. It was on the tip of Gray's tongue to ask him what was wrong when Luke suddenly closed the distance between them. His large body pressed against Gray's as his hands encircled Gray's neck. He used his thumbs to tilt Gray's head up and Gray didn't even have time to let out his gasp of surprise before Luke's mouth closed over his.

The kiss was so gentle and so sweet that Gray actually felt tears burning his eyes. Instead of accepting Gray's parted lips for the invitation they were, Luke brushed his lips over Gray's lower lip first. His mouth was firm and warm and his breath mingled with Gray's as he hung there for just a split second before kissing Gray's upper lip. And then he was skimming over Gray's entire mouth once more before pulling back.

Gray wasn't even aware he'd closed his eyes until he actually opened them and saw Luke's hungry ones staring right back at him. Luke's hands were still cupping his jaw, his thumbs stroking back and forth over his now too hot skin. Gray was about to beg Luke to kiss him again when the elevator dinged. Luke dropped his hands and stepped back as several people got into the car with them. As soon as Luke tore his eyes away and focused on the backs of the people standing in front of them, Gray sucked in a deep breath that left him light-headed. Fortunately, the elevator had several more stops to make before he needed to force himself to move and follow Luke to the truck. Luke didn't say anything as he went around to the driver's side and Gray tried to use the moment to recover from what had been the simplest and most devastating kiss of his entire life.

~

*I*t had been a thousand times better than he ever could have expected. And he didn't regret it for even one second.

Luke kept his attention on the winding road that led up the mountain. It was a shitty excuse to not talk to Gray but even the hour long drive from Missoula had done nothing to ease the knot of emotion that had taken hold deep inside his chest when the doctor had said that one magic word. One word that meant Gray could go back to his life. One word that meant Luke would have to try to figure out his.

Leaving Gray was the only logical option, but just because it was logical didn't mean it would be easy. So he'd made himself a promise in that elevator as Gray had looked to him to confirm that the doctor really had said the tumors were gone. One taste of Gray – it should have been enough to keep his promise to walk away. It should have been but God forgive him, it wasn't.

Darkness was just starting to fall as Luke pulled the truck into Gray's driveway. He reached the front door before Gray did and opened the door to let Ripley out. The dog circled him several times in excitement and then ran to Gray. Gray's hands stroked over the big animal as he said something unintelligible in a low voice. The silky, smooth timbre had Luke's dick swelling even more in his tight jeans and he stepped in the cabin in the hopes of getting himself under control before Gray came in. He heard the door click closed behind him but didn't turn around.

The lack of movement told him Gray was still by the door but Luke couldn't make himself face the other man. He also didn't hear Ripley's nails clicking over the wooden floor so he guessed the dog had stayed outside to explore the yard.

"It was an intense moment, Luke. Emotions were running high… it's just one of those things. It didn't mean anything – I get that. Nothing's changed."

Luke wanted to laugh. Gray actually thought he was regretting the kiss? "For you, Gray?"

"What?"

"Nothing's changed for you?" Luke asked as he finally turned around. "Because everything's changed for me."

Gray was standing just inside the door, his arms wrapped protectively around himself. "I don't know what you want me to say, Luke," he whispered.

"I want you to say that we shouldn't do this…that it will just complicate the fuck out of things."

Gray shook his head. "Not gonna say that."

Luke's insides twisted even as his heart sank because he knew there was no way he was going to be able to keep his promise. He was moving before he could rethink his decision and Gray met him halfway. Their second kiss was the exact opposite of the first and Luke finally gave in as Gray's tongue dueled with his for control. It was a battle he gladly lost because the feel of Gray's tongue sinking into his mouth had Luke moaning deep in his throat as he jammed his hips against the other man's. Gray's long fingers were twisted in his hair to keep him still for his sensual assault but that didn't keep Luke's hands from roaming up and down Gray's back. Even in his weakened state, the feel of Gray's hard body had Luke yearning to explore every inch of him. He managed to get his fingers on the skin at the small of Gray's back and relished how soft it was. But his exploration was cut short when a hand rubbed over his dick and he let out a hoarse groan that Gray immediately swallowed as he continued to plunder Luke's mouth.

Gray palmed his cock over and over as Luke shamelessly thrust against him but when the hand disappeared, Luke let out a ragged, "No."

"Shhhh," Gray said against his lips. "I'm gonna take care of you."

Luke didn't even have time to consider his words because Gray had managed to work his hand beneath Luke's shirt and it coasted over his abdomen before sinking below the waistband of his jeans. The second the hot, rough skin brushed his cock, Luke surged forward to increase the contact. But Gray surprised him with a show of dominance as he used his body to force Luke to take several steps backward. Luke's ass hit the back of the couch and he automatically used one hand to brace himself against it. Gray was quickly working the button and zipper of Luke's jeans free and the fabric didn't even make it past Luke's hips before Gray was on his knees and sucking Luke's swollen dick into his hot, greedy mouth.

~

*G*ray's head was swimming with the sudden turn of events but the second Luke's slick cock slipped past his lips, a surge of clarity went through his entire body. For whatever reason, Luke wanted this...him, and there was no way Gray was going to fuck it up, even if not every part of his body was along for the ride. He'd had a little bit of hope left that his dick might respond to the feeling of Luke's heavy hands roaming over his body but it hadn't. The rest of Gray's body was drawn tight with need and that fiery heat that started deep in his belly and burned through all four limbs was there but his cock had let him down – both figuratively and literally. But at this point, just the feel of Luke surrounding him...joining with him, was enough.

He let his tongue explore the ridges of Luke's shaft before sucking on the head. Luke was thicker and longer than most of the men he'd been with so it took him a while to work all of Luke deep into his throat. But once he had him there, he swallowed and the resulting moan of approval from above had him doing it again. He could feel Luke's hands cradling his head and there was something incredibly erotic in the way the calloused fingertips scratched over his scalp. But what turned him on more than anything was the way Luke whispered his name with a mixture of awe and need.

Gray let his hands settle on Luke's tight ass and couldn't stop himself from massaging the globes. It was probably more than he should have done to someone who hadn't ever experienced a man's touch before but Luke didn't seem to have any issue with it because he quickly got Gray's unspoken message and began to thrust into Gray's mouth. Grunts of pure bliss spilled from Luke's mouth as Gray twisted his tongue around his shaft with every forward motion but then Luke did something Gray hadn't been expecting. He pulled free of Gray's mouth and leaned down to seal their lips together. This time it was Gray's mouth that was worshipped and when Luke finally released him, Gray momentarily forgot his primary intent because he got lost in Luke's hungry gaze.

"I knew it would be like this," Luke murmured as his thumb trailed over Gray's lower lip.

"Like what?" Gray whispered.

"Like finding something I didn't know was missing."

The words had Gray spellbound for several long seconds and then his hungry mouth was sucking Luke's cock into its depths. He showed Luke no mercy as he licked, sucked and nipped the sensitive flesh and when he heard Luke roar in satisfaction, he sealed his mouth around the spasming flesh between his lips and swallowed as jet after endless jet of semen hit the back of his throat. Long after Luke's orgasm eased, Gray sucked on the crown of Luke's cock until there was nothing left and then he rose to his feet and drew Luke against him for a searing kiss.

~

*L*uke never would have thought the taste of his own come would be a turn-on but with Gray's mouth as the delivery system, he couldn't get enough. As wrung out as he was from the explosive orgasm that he'd felt in every cell of his body, Luke was eager to reciprocate and reached one hand out to stroke over Gray's groin. But before he could make contact, Gray was stepping back and saying, "We should check on Ripley."

The brush-off stung but Luke released the grip he had on Gray's waist. "Okay."

He couldn't read the look in Gray's eyes as he put more distance between them but when Gray murmured, "You know, I think I'm just going to call it a night," Luke could only nod because all the pleasure he'd felt just a moment before turned into something cold and ugly inside of him.

"Did I do something wrong?" he heard himself asking before he could think better of it. He hated the vulnerability in his voice but he hated the idea of not knowing what he'd done to make Gray do such a 180 more.

"No, just tired," Gray said with ill-concealed sheepishness. "See you in the morning."

Luke watched Gray turn his back on him and disappear down the hall leading to his room. It took everything in him not to follow and demand an explanation so he ended up going outside instead. He spent a good half an hour walking around the property as the sun finally slipped behind the horizon but not even the chill in the air could calm his raging frustration. Luke had had his fair share of blowjobs from the few women he'd dated but none could come close to what Gray had done to him. With the women it had only felt like they were slaking some physical need inside him but with Gray it had felt like so much more. He'd seen the look in Gray's eyes when he'd told Gray how he felt – he'd fucking felt it in Gray's touch...you couldn't fake that shit.

It was that thought that had Luke storming back into the cabin and going straight for Gray's room. He threw open the door only to find that Gray wasn't asleep. He was sitting fully dressed on his bed looking at his tablet.

"You owe me more!" Luke growled as he stomped into the room and tore the tablet from Gray's hands. "You can't just fucking rip my world apart and then come in here and disappear into one of your books that you love so much-"

Luke's rant died a quick death when he glanced at the tablet and saw what Gray had been looking at. "What is this?" he asked as he scanned the title of the article. *Sex after Testicular Cancer – What You Need to Know.*

"Nothing," Gray mumbled as he stood and tried to push past Luke.

Luke grabbed him with his free hand. "Is this why you walked away from me?" he asked as he held the tablet up.

Gray dropped his gaze. "The doctor said that the testosterone I was taking would help me get it up..."

Gray's voice dropped off as he tried to pull free of Luke's hold. Understanding dawned and Luke tossed the tablet on the bed. "You didn't feel anything out there."

"I felt things with you I've never felt before but not anywhere where I could do something about it," Gray admitted. He glanced at the tablet. "I was hoping to find some other things I could try..." he began to say but then shook his head. Luke didn't miss the flood of color in his cheeks.

Luke hated how tense Gray was so he did the only thing he could think of and kissed him long and deep. Gray's answering moan had Luke shouting a silent victory cry in his mind and then he was pushing Gray down on the bed and pinning him in place with his body. His own dick was already rock hard again and he nearly cried out in relief when Gray opened his legs to make room for him.

"Our bodies line up perfectly," Luke whispered as he peppered Gray's face with light kisses. He could feel Gray's hands at his waist and they tightened at Luke's words. "I just want to explore you, Gray. If that's all we do tonight or the next night..."

Luke realized he was treading into dangerous territory with his talk of a future that didn't exist so he switched gears and settled deeper into the cradle of Gray's hips and then kissed him. "Tell me it's okay," he finally said when he came up for air.

Gray nodded but then he was trying to sit up. "Let me just turn off the lights," Gray said as he struggled under Luke's greater weight.

"No, I want to see all of you," Luke said as he easily subdued Gray and gently held his arms down.

Tears formed in Gray's eyes and Luke instantly relinquished his hold on Gray but Gray just lay unmoving beneath him. "I'm a freak, Luke," he cried out suddenly. "Even when my hair grows back and I gain weight, I'll still only be half a man."

Gray looked so broken as silent tears streaked down his cheeks that Luke was on the verge of releasing him entirely. But his instincts kicked in and he stayed where he was and leaned down and began kissing away the salty tears until they stopped all together. Gray's body eventually went pliant beneath his and his ragged breaths eased. And when Luke kissed his mouth, Gray kissed him back.

"Do you feel that, Gray?" Luke murmured as he rubbed his erection against Gray's body. "So even if you don't believe the words I'm about to say, believe this, because my body can't lie and it knows exactly who it wants," Luke said.

"I knew the day we met that I wanted you in a way I've never wanted another person, man or woman. And I knew when I talked to Dane and Jax that this need I have wasn't about any man, it was about one man. It's you and only you. Nothing about you is a turn-off for me. Nothing."

He leaned down to brush a kiss across Gray's lips. "I'll stop the moment you tell me to but make sure it's because you don't want me because I won't accept anything less."

Luke was thrilled when Gray initiated the next kiss. It quickly went from tentative and uncertain to needy and raw and it was Luke who had to break the kiss to catch his breath. Gray's hands had found their way under his shirt and were skimming up and down his back as his hips lifted so he was brushing Luke's cock with every upward motion.

With his desire quickly spiraling out of control, Luke reared back and stripped off his shirt and then went to work on the buttons of Gray's. His fingers felt too big and awkward for the task and as his eyes connected with Gray's he said, "See what you do to me?"

His voice sounded husky even to his own ears. But Gray seemed to understand his dilemma because he sat up and with Luke now straddling him, began helping with the buttons. Luke abandoned the task and focused on kissing Gray instead. Once Gray finished with the last button, he stilled his hands and Luke knew he was struggling with the final step of baring his body completely.

"Show me," Luke whispered against Gray's lips.

Gray removed the shirt slowly and tossed it to the floor and then his hands dropped down to rest on Luke's thighs. Luke let his fingers explore Gray's smooth skin. While Gray had definitely lost some muscle definition, it didn't deter Luke in the least as he explored every ridge and hollow. He let his fingers settle on the spot on Gray's chest where he'd struck him that first day.

"It feels like a lifetime ago, doesn't it?" Luke asked softly.

"I never would have guessed that one of the worst days in my life would also be one of the best," Gray said.

Luke hung there for a moment as he absorbed the words and then he was pushing Gray back down on the bed and devouring his mouth. Gray's eager tongue welcomed Luke as he thrust past Gray's full lips. They kissed for several long minutes until Luke finally forced himself to release Gray's mouth and scorched a trail of kisses down Gray's neck. His fingers roamed over Gray's chest and settled on his nipples. He played with one while he sucked at the point where Gray's neck and shoulder met and he heard a strangled moan escape Gray's lips. An assault on Gray's nipples was next and the resulting whimpers had Luke grinding his dick mindlessly against Gray's.

As Luke made his way down Gray's body, he felt Gray begin to tense up. The reaction helped cool Luke's raging need and he shifted back up so he could kiss Gray. "Move up a little," he said softly. Gray hesitated - probably because he knew why Luke wanted him to move farther up the bed – but then eased himself up on to his elbows and pulled himself up closer to the headboard and when he was done moving, Luke settled over him once more.

"One word and this stops, Gray. I just need to be with you even if that means all we do is sleep-"

Gray sat up and kissed him before he could finish the sentence and then he was taking Luke's hand in his and placing it over the button on his pants. He lowered himself back down to the bed and watched Luke as Luke slowly worked the button free. The zipper was next and then Luke was climbing off of Gray so he could pull Gray's pants off of him. He left Gray's underwear where it was and focused his attention on the rest of Gray's body. He kissed and touched every surface he could reach and when he next looked up to see if Gray was okay, he was glad to see that Gray's eyes were closed and his lower lip was caught between his teeth.

Luke let his hands brush over Gray's still flaccid cock and the instant he did, all the tension he'd managed to work out of Gray's body came back and his eyes flew open. Luke palmed Gray's dick as their eyes held each other but he didn't make a move to remove Gray's underwear until Gray gave him an almost imperceptible nod. Gray lifted his hips long enough to allow Luke to lower the underwear but he didn't remove them entirely because his gaze was focused on Gray's cock.

A moment of uncertainty came over him as the full impact of what he was about to do hit him. He'd loved what Gray had done to him out in the living room but getting a blowjob and giving one were two very different things. What if he hated it and couldn't go through with it? What kind of damage would that do to Gray's vulnerable psyche? But even as his doubt began to build, he was reminded of the trust Gray had put in him – this one chance he'd given Luke to show him that he wasn't any less of a man.

With that thought in mind, Luke reached down to run his tongue over the surprisingly soft skin. Intrigued, he did it again and then once more and with each caress, he felt saliva start to flood his mouth as his lust exploded. Whatever apprehension he felt at touching a man so intimately faded to the back of his mind as he ran his tongue over the crown. Gray surged beneath him at the contact so Luke did it again. As he continued to explore Gray's length, he heard a cry of distress and looked up to see Gray had covered his eyes with his hands.

Instead of asking Gray if he wanted him to stop, Luke used his hand to pull Gray's dick away from his body. He ignored the fold of empty skin beneath the heavy flesh and sealed his mouth over the tip. With each subsequent suck, he drew more of Gray's length into his mouth and a surge of energy went through him when he felt the hot flesh twitch against his tongue. Gray had gone deathly quiet and Luke didn't dare look up to check on him because he couldn't bear to see the man's disappointment. As he continued to massage Gray's cock, Luke slipped his palm under Gray's ass to knead the flesh and then his finger was slipping between the crease to search out his hole. He brushed over the pulsing entrance several times and then removed his finger. Instead of putting his finger in his mouth, he reached up to press it against Gray's lips.

At some point he'd gotten Gray's attention because Gray was watching him with a mix of desperation and want and he instantly opened his mouth and sucked Luke's finger in. The pressure Gray exerted on his digit had Luke remembering what it felt like to have the man's mouth wrapped around him and he instantly changed the level of tension he was applying to Gray's dick. A hiss escaped from Gray's mouth as he released Luke's finger and Luke nearly cried out at the feel of Gray's dick thickening in his mouth. Luke kept up the torment and used his finger to find Gray's opening once more. Gray's saliva eased the way and as soon as his finger pushed past the outer muscle trying to deny Luke's entry, Gray's dick swelled even more.

"Luke!" Gray called out and another glance up showed he had Gray's complete attention.

Luke pulled his finger back out and then pressed it in again until he was in as far as he could go. Gray began to alternate between pushing up into his mouth and trying to bear down even farther onto his finger. Luke stroked over Gray's inner walls until he found the bundle of nerves he was looking for. Gray actually shouted at the contact and then he began thrusting heavily into Luke's mouth as his cock hardened to the point that Luke could no longer keep him fully in his mouth without gagging. Luke made sure to strike Gray's prostate over and over again with his finger as he continued sucking on Gray, and Luke's own lust was so intense that he began humping his hips into the bed. A sudden curse erupted from Gray's mouth and then he was jerking against Luke uncontrollably and while there was no fluid to accompany Gray's orgasm, the feel of his dick pulsing inside of Luke's mouth had Luke's own body responding and he swallowed the moan that erupted as he came.

Several long seconds passed as Luke tried to catch his breath which was made all the harder since he wasn't ready to release Gray's still twitching dick or remove his finger from the man's rippling ass. Luke gently sucked on Gray as they both came down and then finally pulled his finger free of Gray's body and let his cock go after giving it one final lick. Ignoring the liquid seeping through his underwear and jeans, Luke climbed up Gray's body. Gray's eyes were closed and he was quiet...so quiet that Luke actually felt a moment of panic that he'd somehow inadvertently hurt him.

"Gray..."

Gray's eyes slowly opened and the sight of unshed tears had Luke reaching for his face. "Oh God, did I hurt you?"

Gray quickly shook his head and even as the tears fell, he reached up and palmed Luke's cheek. Relief went through Luke but it was short-lived because nothing could have prepared him for the moment when Gray suddenly whispered, "I love you, Luke."

CHAPTER 8

"Will you tell me about this?" Gray asked as he trailed his fingers over the scar that started at Luke's temple and disappeared into his hair. He'd been petting Luke for a while now, ever since he'd woken up to find Luke lying across his chest. Almost thirty minutes had passed before he'd felt Luke's breathing change enough to indicate he was awake and Gray had used the time to think back to the night before after he'd let those three words slip from his lips. Luke hadn't responded to his declaration other than to kiss him long and deep but there'd been a moment after Luke climbed off of him and disappeared into the bathroom that Gray was sure he'd fucked up to the point that he'd lost Luke. But Luke had come back within a minute, minus his jeans and underwear and he'd crawled under the covers next to Gray and dragged him up against his chest.

Luke tensed in his arms but didn't move otherwise except to drag his fingers back and forth over Gray's side where he was holding him. His ear was pressed to Gray's chest and he could only imagine that Luke could feel his racing heart.

"It happened last fall. My unit was on a mission in this village just outside Kabul. There'd been intelligence that a high value Taliban leader was hiding out there with his family so we were supposed to go in and find him."

"Did you?"

Luke shook his head. "We broke up into two man teams to sweep the residences but when we couldn't raise our Staff Sergeant and the Private he was with, my buddy Eddie and I went to check on them."

Luke was quiet for so long that Gray asked, "What happened?"

Luke shook his head. "It was over so fast. We were clearing the residence Staff Sergeant Shaw and Private Barnes had been in and then Eddie was gone. Then I got hit. I woke up in a hospital in Germany a week later with no memory of that night."

"Your colleagues?"

"Were fine. Barnes was there when I woke up and told me his and Shaw's Comms had gone down and they'd already cleared the house. He said an insurgent must have come in afterwards…"

"I'm sorry, Luke."

"Eddie was twenty-two years old. His girlfriend had just given birth to their daughter a couple weeks earlier and he was planning to ask her to marry him on his next leave."

Gray tightened his arms around Luke since he doubted anything he said would help him make sense of the tragedy.

"What happened after that? Did you go home or back to Afghanistan?"

"Home. It was our unit's last mission for that deployment so my team was already back in the States by the time I got back. Barnes accompanied me home. About a week after I got back I went to see Eddie's girlfriend. She lived in a small apartment off base and had decided to move back to Arizona to be closer to her family. I was helping her load up some stuff into her car when the first flashback hit me."

Gray tensed. "From that night?"

Luke nodded. "I didn't realize what it was at first – just some voices, a gun-shot, Eddie falling. The doctors had said not to expect my memory of that night to return so I kind of just passed it off as a one-time thing. But it kept happening. Flashes here and there that I couldn't make sense of."

The tension in Luke's frame was telling and Gray said, "You remembered all of it, didn't you?"

Another nod.

"Tell me," Gray urged.

"All of it came back to me in a rush one night about six weeks ago."

Right before Luke had shown up on the side of the road outside Dare.

"When Eddie and I were clearing that house, we heard voices – yelling. We recognized the man's voice as Staff Sergeant Shaw's so we followed it to this back room. Shaw and Barnes were standing over this woman and her three kids who were all on their knees. Shaw was convinced she was the wife of the man we'd been looking for and he was screaming at her to tell him where the guy was. She was crying and saying she didn't know who they were talking about."

Luke's voice cracked and Gray stroked a hand over his shoulder. "Then Shaw pulls out his gun and shoots the first kid. A little boy – not even three years old. I shouted at him and then Eddie falls to the ground. I got hit next. After I fell, I saw Shaw point his gun at the next kid and then everything went dark."

Understanding dawned and Gray felt the bottom of his stomach drop out. "They're the ones who're after you."

"Shaw is. After my memory came back, I went to Barnes' place to confront him – he'd been by my side the whole time I was in the hospital and he became like my shadow when I got back. I thought he was just trying to be a good friend at the time."

"He was watching you to see if your memory came back."

"He and Shaw left me in that house thinking I was dead. Some guys from my team found me and Eddie when they couldn't reach us on our Comms. After I realized it was Barnes and Shaw, I went to Barnes' apartment. I found him lying on the floor in his living room in a pool of blood. I was checking for a pulse when Shaw walked in from a back bedroom. When he saw me he actually laughed and said I was saving him a step. Then he pulled a gun on me and asked me if it looked familiar."

"It was your gun?" Gray asked as everything began to fall into place.

Luke nodded. "He or Barnes must have taken it off me at some point after I was shot."

"He used it to kill Barnes, didn't he?"

"My fingerprints all over a weapon that belonged to me..."

"Fuck," Gray muttered.

"I managed to get the drop on Shaw but he got a shot off before I could get out of there."

Gray's fingers automatically sought out the scar on Luke's side – the one he had helped stitch up.

"I barely had time to get back to my place to get some stuff before the MPs – Military Police - showed up. I didn't know how many other members of my team were in on it with Shaw so I took off. I'd seen the story about Rhys a few days earlier and I knew he was the only one I could trust."

"And then you saw that he was a cop again."

"He'd have no choice but to turn me in," Luke said quietly.

Gray managed to keep his touch soothing but inside he was burning with frustration and helplessness. "Why did he do this?"

Luke seemed to know what Gray was asking because he said, "The terrorist we were looking for was on the top of the FBI's Most Wanted Terrorists list – he was their lead suspect in that New Year's day bombing in New York."

"I remember that – three people died," Gray murmured.

"Shaw was talking about how bagging him would launch his career. He had all these plans to run for political office when his enlistment ended later this year – the Senate I think. Turned out the woman and kids he killed weren't even related to the guy we were looking for."

"You're the only witness..." Gray said.

"As far as I know. I don't know how many of the other members of my unit knew what Shaw was up to. Barnes was young and impressionable so I keep hoping he was the only one, but I just don't know," Luke said tiredly.

Gray held Luke for a moment longer and then gently rolled him onto his back and settled on top of him. "I'm sorry, Luke. I know how much they meant to you."

"They were all I had."

"Not all," Gray whispered as he leaned down and kissed Luke. He pulled back enough so his eyes could connect with Luke's. "I meant what I said last night."

Luke tensed beneath him.

"I don't expect you to say it back but I don't want you to think I just said it in the heat of the moment."

Luke's hand came up to cup his cheek. "You've been through a lot these past few weeks, Gray. It's only natural for you to get attached to me..."

Gray tried to ignore the sting of pain that went through him at Luke's words. "I haven't been sure of anything since the day the doctor told me the life I'd been living was over. I'm sure of this," Gray said firmly as he brushed a soft kiss over Luke's lips.

"I love everything you did for me but that's not why I love you." He kissed Luke again but this time it lasted much longer and he could feel Luke's body responding. Gray skimmed his fingers down over Luke's face and neck and then stopped just over his heart. "I've based my entire career on being able to find the right words, but I'm so scared right now that nothing I say will make you believe me," Gray whispered.

Luke's hand wrapped around the back of his neck and pulled him down until their lips were nearly touching. "I believe you, Gray. No one's ever said those words to me," Luke admitted before tightening his grip. "No one," he repeated firmly.

Gray wanted so badly to tell Luke he'd spend the rest of their lives telling him he loved him but the idea of Luke shooting down the idea of them having a future together was too painful to deal with so Gray settled his mouth on Luke's instead and hoped Luke would feel and taste everything he wasn't able to put into words.

～

*L*uke sank farther into the bedding as Gray's mouth dotted his jaw with soft kisses. He was still reeling from Gray's admission and while he hadn't let himself believe the words last night after Gray had said them, he believed them now. It was written all over Gray's face and in every touch, every caress. Emotion clogged Luke's throat as Gray worshipped him but when Gray sucked him deep into his mouth, Luke lost the ability to think. The sensual torture went on and on as Gray took him to the brink over and over again. Luke's whole body felt hot and itchy and overly sensitive and he couldn't stop himself from whispering, "Gray, please."

But instead of sending him over the edge, Gray released him and worked his way up Luke's body and sought out Luke's lips. A thrill shot through Luke when he felt Gray's erection rubbing against his.

"Make love to me, Luke," Gray said.

Luke could only manage a nod and he carefully rolled Gray onto his back. Gray made a move for the nightstand drawer but Luke stopped him and made sure Gray was focused on him. "I do, you know," he said quietly. "Love you," he added at Gray's questioning look.

Joy lit up Gray's face and Luke kissed him softly. Gray reached to pull a condom and lube from the nightstand and Luke's whole body seized up. "I've never...I don't want to hurt you," he admitted.

"You won't," Gray reassured him. "Just go slow, okay? It's been a while for me."

Luke nodded and then took the condom and placed it farther down the bed. His fingers shook as Gray squeezed some lube on them. He watched as Gray pulled his legs up and apart and the sight of Gray's opening had his dick jerking hard against his abdomen. As much as he wanted to spend time just exploring Gray, Luke knew he was already at his limit so he swiped some of the lube over the fluttering hole and then began to work one finger inside his lover. Whimpers of pleasure began falling from Gray's lips as his body sucked Luke's finger in. He massaged Gray's inner walls a bit before pulling his finger out and carefully adding a second. As he waited for

Gray's body to adjust, his eyes sought out Gray's and the stark beauty in the other man's expression had Luke shifting so that he could kiss him.

"Next time I'm going to taste your pretty little hole," Luke murmured against Gray's lips and Gray's whole body jerked in response and his body clamped down on Luke's finger. Luke began fucking Gray with his fingers at the same time that he fucked his mouth with his tongue. The carnality of it had Gray writhing against him as he desperately tried to get some relief but just as he sensed Gray's imminent release, Luke removed his fingers. It took him precious seconds to get the condom on and he added some more lube for good measure but the sight of Gray's parted lips and glazed over eyes had Luke biting back a curse as he fumbled to get into position. As he lined his dick up with Gray's entrance, he looked up to watch Gray so he could gauge his reactions. And he was glad he did because the second his crown breached Gray's body, Gray arched his back and pressed his head into the pillows as a groan of blissful agony tore through him.

Although Luke's intent had been to go slow, Gray wasn't as patient and he began pushing against Luke's dick without any hesitation. The heat and pressure that welcomed Luke as he slid all the way home had him calling Gray's name, and then his body took over and he began thrusting in and out in long, powerful glides. He sat back on his heels and pulled Gray up enough so that he could watch his swollen cock disappear into Gray's body. The sight was so overwhelming that he couldn't help but look up at Gray in wonder. "So fucking beautiful," he whispered.

Gray shifted up on his elbows so he could watch but it wasn't enough for Luke so he wrapped his arms around Gray and lifted him so that Gray was riding him. The position had Gray sinking farther down on Luke and he heard Gray's cry of approval against his shoulder where Gray had buried his face. With every upward thrust, Gray dropped all his weight down to meet Luke's greedy cock. And the second Luke started to pull out, Gray's inner muscles clamped down on him to try to hold him in place.

"I love you so much, Luke," Gray moaned against his ear and then Gray's lips were on his. Their tongues matched the desperate pace their bodies had set and Luke struggled to get one hand between them to search out Gray's dick. It was hard and hot and heavy in his hand so Luke began ruthlessly jerking him off in the hopes that they'd be able to come as close together as possible. And seconds later, his wish was granted because Gray shouted against his mouth and then jammed his hips down hard on Luke's cock. His channel pulsed around Luke which set off Luke's own orgasm. Shards of white hot pleasure shot to all of Luke's limbs as the coil that had wrapped tight deep inside of him snapped free and flung him over the edge. Gray's fingers curled into his back as his body began to jerk uncontrollably in Luke's arms and his dick convulsed in Luke's hand.

Minutes passed as aftershocks continued to rock through them and it took every last bit of Luke's strength to lower them both to the bed so that his body was covering Gray's. He felt Gray's legs wrap around him and draw so tight that it forced his cock even deeper into his lover's body. Soft kisses were pressed against his collarbone as Gray's stranglehold on his neck finally eased and then Gray was pulling him down for a deep kiss that stole what little reserve energy he had left.

～

*A*s Luke began pumping into him from behind, Gray sent another prayer of thanks that he'd had enough foresight to grab a condom and the lube before climbing into the shower. He hadn't been sure if Luke would join him after he'd gone to let Ripley out and get the coffee started but within 5 minutes, Luke had been pushing the shower curtain aside and forcing Gray back against the tile and pinning his arms to the wall as he stole his breath with a bone melting kiss. Gray had been almost certain that there was no way he'd be able to get another hard-on after the passionate encounter in his bed only half an hour earlier but the second Luke had spun him around and pushed his finger into Gray's body, Gray's dick had gone from relaxed to half hard. One stroke over his prostate and Gray had been rubbing his dick against the tile in a desperate effort to find some relief.

He was still stunned that he'd even managed to get hard when Luke had first put his mouth on him the night before but he'd found that the more his anxiety over Luke seeing his cock without the expected heavy sack beneath eased, the more his dick had actually responded. His doctor had told him early on that with testosterone he could have a normal sex life after surgery but that his mental hang-ups over the changes to his body could actually be more of a deterrent than his physical limitations. He'd suggested Gray talk to a counselor or talk to other patients who'd been through the same thing but Gray had been so caught up in what he'd lost, he hadn't even considered it. And if Luke hadn't been patient but insistent in his exploration of Gray's body last night, who knows how long Gray would have missed out?

As for Luke, any first time jitters he might have had about fucking a man had appeared to have flown out the window at this point because he teased Gray mercilessly by sliding his dick between Gray's cheeks while keeping his hands on Gray's hips to make sure he couldn't rub himself off. Every time the head of Luke's cock had brushed over his hole, Gray had pushed back and begged Luke to fuck him but Luke had ignored him. At one point, Gray had become so desperate that he reached for his dick to bring about his own release but Luke had grabbed both his hands and pinned them over his head against the wall. The feeling of being immobilized and at Luke's mercy had gotten Gray harder than he'd ever been before in his life and when Luke finally did shove his dick into him, Gray came on the first thrust. He'd expected Luke to take his own pleasure at that point but he'd merely hung there inside of Gray's body as he began whispering in Gray's ear about some of the things he wanted to do to him. To Gray's absolute shock, he'd felt his dick responding again. But it wasn't until his dick was standing at full attention against his stomach that Luke began pumping into him again.

"So tight," Luke muttered against his ear. Gray's hands were still pinned but when Luke said, "Leave them there" and then released them, Gray didn't dare move them. Instead, he laid his palms flat on the tile and braced himself as Luke's lunges began to shove him forward. Luke's hands stroked over his entire body and then settled on his nipples. He tortured them with a few hard tugs and then moved his palms down to Gray's thighs. Hard fingers bit into his skin and forced his legs farther apart and then held them that way as Luke ruthlessly slammed into him. Hoarse cries fell from Gray's mouth as he pressed his cheek against the wall. His need to come was so intense that it bordered on pain and he didn't even realize he was begging Luke until Luke whispered, "Not yet, baby. Just a little more."

At that point Gray lost all sense of time as well as his surroundings. He couldn't feel the water anymore or even the smooth tile that was acting as a counterpoint to Luke's nearly brutal thrusts. The only thing he felt was the fiery burning in his ass and the unyielding pressure in his dick. And the spire of need that drew tighter and tighter every time Luke hammered into him.

"One day, there won't be anything separating us," Luke suddenly growled.

"Do it," Gray ordered, his voice barely a whisper. But Luke must have heard him because his pace slowed slightly. "I'm negative, I swear," Gray ground out.

Luke stopped all together and Gray nearly cried out at the feeling of loss even though Luke was still inside of him. But suddenly Luke pulled out but before Gray could even register the loss, Luke was slamming back into him and he nearly cried out at the feel of Luke's bare skin scorching his insides. Any control Luke might have had was gone as he shoved Gray forward until he was flush with the wall and then fucked him without mercy. It took just seconds for Gray's body to get back to where it was and without any warning at all, he was thrown over the chasm of pleasure and began falling as wave after wave of ecstasy tore through him. Fire burned his inner walls as Luke came inside of him and he felt the other man's fingers biting into his shoulders, holding him in place while he humped into him.

Luke's orgasm went on and on as he jerked into Gray over and over and Gray relished the feel of Luke's release warming him from the inside out. When Luke's movements finally slowed and then stopped all together, Gray turned his head to look over his shoulder and was met with a hungry kiss that left him shaking. Luke's rumble of laughter felt good against his back and when Luke slipped free of his body, he tried to turn around. But Luke's big palm settled on his back to hold him in place and it wasn't until the come began dripping from his ass that Gray realized why Luke wasn't letting him turn around. If he wasn't thoroughly exhausted, the idea of Luke watching his seed drip from Gray's body would have gotten Gray hard all over again. So Gray waited until Luke took in his fill and then turned him around. Luke kissed him for a good long time before he reached for the body wash to help Gray finish his shower.

~

"Stop it," Luke heard Gray mutter.

"What?" Luke asked, feigning innocence.

"You said you wanted to read one of my books, so read," Gray growled. But the fact that Gray was shifting in his chair had Luke smiling since the man was no doubt thinking the same exact thing Luke had been thinking.

Luke forced his eyes back down to the book in his hands but as before, he'd only managed to read a few sentences before he was looking up to watch Gray again. It was the exact same scenario that had set Luke off only an hour earlier when he'd come into the living room to find Gray typing away at his computer. His intent at the time had only been to give Gray a quick kiss in greeting before letting Gray get back to his writing but one kiss had led to another and then another and then Gray had been shoving his laptop out of the way while Luke had torn at his clothes. They'd started off with Gray bent over the desk but Luke had wanted to see him when he came so he'd rolled him to his back and dragged his ass to the edge of the desk before ramming into him again. Gray had come first so Luke had gotten exactly what he wanted. Luke's orgasm had quickly followed and then he'd dragged Gray to the shower to get cleaned up. After that, Luke had planned to head outside to give Gray some space so he could get some work done but a downpour had changed that and he'd asked Gray if he could read one of his books instead.

"You know, pretty soon I'm going to take it personally that you can't keep your attention on my book."

Luke chuckled. "I can guarantee that there isn't a book or even movie on this earth that I would ever choose over your ass."

Gray smiled and shook his head. "You sweet talker."

Luke laughed and then got up. "I'll be in the bedroom if you need me," he said as he went to the desk to give Gray a quick kiss. But Gray's gaze was focused on the screen and when Luke glanced at it, he saw why. A picture of Gray and a man kissing was on the screen and the headline above the picture read, *Bestselling Author Gray Hawthorne Accused of Sexual Harassment.*

"What the fuck?" Luke snapped as he grabbed the laptop so he could get a better look. Rage went through him at the sight of Gray in the other man's arms. "What is this?" he asked Gray who'd gone pale.

Since Gray wasn't responding, Luke hit the play button that was in the middle of the picture and the video launched as a female reporter began speaking.

"The entertainment world was rocked with a bombshell accusation by actor Christian Cavelli today. After weeks of silence after pictures surfaced of Cavelli and bestselling author, Gray Hawthorne, in an intimate embrace, Cavelli has admitted that Hawthorne attempted to force the young heart-throb into a sexual relationship in exchange for landing the leading role in the upcoming film trilogy based on Hawthorne's bestselling Nick Archer series. With his fiancée, Deanna Tate, at his side, Cavelli tearfully explained how he was forced to choose between the role that would have rocketed him to superstardom and his convictions."

The image switched to a good looking young man holding a very pregnant woman's hand. *"I hope that by coming forward I can help others who've faced this same struggle. No one in a position of power has the right to force someone else-"*

Disgusted, Luke slammed the laptop shut.

"Luke, I swear, I didn't-"

"Gray, don't you fucking dare think I believe the horseshit coming from that guy's mouth!"

Gray looked taken aback by Luke's words. "Is this the scandal Dane was talking about?"

"Yes and no; back then it was just the pictures. Christian's camp never commented on them and neither did I so the press just came to the conclusion that we were having an affair. But we weren't," Gray quickly added. "He auditioned for the lead role a couple months back. The studio liked him for the part but my contract says I have to sign off on anyone they choose for the lead and I knew Christian wasn't right for it – he was too young and I just wasn't impressed by his take on the character. He showed up at my house a couple days later and begged me to reconsider but I wouldn't. I was showing him out when he kissed me. I stopped it right away and told him to go but I guess there must have been some paparazzi following him because the pictures showed up the next day."

"He used them to try to blackmail you, didn't he?" Luke said.

Gray nodded. "He told me if I didn't sign off on him for the part, he'd tell everyone I propositioned him for sex in exchange for the part. I told him to fuck off. He tried strong-arming the studio a couple weeks ago with a lawsuit but the only thing they can do at this point is call off the whole deal – they'd be out tens of millions of dollars since pre-production has already started and they'd still have to pay me whether the movies get made or not."

"You need to make some kind of statement or something – tell them your side," Luke argued.

Gray rose to his feet and pushed past him. "There's no point – people are going to believe what they want to believe."

"What does that mean?"

Gray whirled around. "Don't you get it, Luke? I'm the bad guy and he" – Gray pointed at the laptop – "is their do-no-wrong, golden boy. I played the game and I lost. And you know the really fucked up part?" Gray bit out. "I'm still going to sell a shitload of books because of this. The studio's going to make all the money they projected and then some and Cavelli – he'll probably get an even better role handed to him."

Luke shook his head. "So you're okay with them believing the lie?"

"They'll believe it because that's what they want to believe. I'm on top and that means they need to knock me down a few pegs. There's blood in the water now and nothing I say will change that. And you know what? For the first time in a really long time, I don't give a shit. Hell, I'm almost glad because I don't have to keep pretending anymore. All I ever wanted to do was write – the rest of this all just happened and yeah, I got sucked in. But right now, being here in this place, being here with you – this is the moment I was praying to God for while we were waiting for Dr. Klein to tell us if I was in remission or not - not my career, not some movie deal, not Cavelli keeping his mouth shut!"

A rush of emotion went through Luke and he tossed the book onto the couch and went to Gray and began rubbing his hands up and down Gray's arms. "I love you, Gray. But I don't want you to risk your entire career for something that won't…"

"Last," Gray finished for him.

"There are only two ways this can end. I prove Shaw was behind everything or Shaw finds me."

Gray pulled free of him. "I don't accept that! I don't!" he shouted once more before he turned and headed towards the bedroom. Luke knew he should follow him but since he couldn't figure out what to say to make Gray see the truth that what they had wasn't meant to be, he snatched the car keys off the kitchen table and left the cabin.

CHAPTER 9

*G*ray heard the diesel engine cut out and the front door open but he wasn't surprised when heavy footsteps passed his bedroom by. It had been nearly two weeks since he and Luke had made love the night after Gray's test results had proved he was for the moment, cancer free. And not once in those two weeks had Luke spent the night in his own room. It was a sign that even now, Luke was pulling away from him – preparing him for a future Gray had no way to prevent.

Rolling onto his side, Gray tried to hold back the tears that threatened. Life really was a cruel bitch. He'd managed to beat a brutal medical diagnosis and treatment but he was going to end up losing his life anyway because he wasn't sure he could survive in a future that didn't include Luke. No way in hell could he go back to being the shell of the man he'd been before Luke walked into his life and changed it forever. He'd been surrounded by people, had more money than he'd known what to do with and had countless men to slake his lusts on but he'd never once managed to feel any different than the little boy who'd locked himself in his room to escape his parents' cruel tirades and angry rants. His books had provided the escape he'd needed then and later his writing had given him the voice he hadn't been able to find as a child but it was being with Luke that made him feel like he was exactly where he was supposed to be. Cancer could steal his health and Hollywood could take back the glory it'd bestowed on him but Luke...without Luke he was nothing.

Gray tensed when he heard his door open but he didn't look up. His back was to Luke when he felt his mattress dip under Luke's weight and he managed to stifle a cry of relief when he felt Luke curl up against his back. Luke's arm wrapped around his waist and Gray reached down to pull Luke's hand up so it was resting over his heart and he laced their fingers together.

"Sorry," he heard Luke whisper against his neck and then soft lips were brushing over his skin.

"You can't say shit like that to me and just expect me to be okay with it," Gray whispered.

"Even with all the crap your career comes with-"

Gray quickly rolled over. "I'm talking about what you said about Shaw finding you – you can't ask me to just accept your death as some fucking foregone conclusion," he said harshly.

He expected Luke to put up some kind of argument or try to reason with him but Luke remained silent. His big fingers brushed Gray's cheeks and the sight of moisture on the end of Luke's thumb had Gray realizing he hadn't managed to stem his tears.

"There's this form that you have to fill out when you join the military – it's for who they should notify if you don't make it out. I put Rhys' name down when I first filled it out but they wanted me to put down the name of someone who wasn't actively enlisted."

"You didn't have anyone?" Gray guessed.

Luke shook his head. "I made up a name because I was too embarrassed to tell them there was no one else who would care if I came home or not."

"What name did you put?"

"Elizabeth Saint."

"Why that one?"

"Because that was the name of the hospital my mom left me at. St. Elizabeth's in Chicago."

"She left you there?"

"In a box underneath a waiting room chair. I wasn't even an hour old."

"They never found her?" Gray asked as he shifted closer to Luke.

"No one even remembered seeing her," Luke said. "The only thing I know about her is that she cared enough about me not to leave me in a dumpster somewhere but not enough to leave a note saying why she didn't want me or even what my name was."

"Is that when you were placed in a group home?"

Luke shook his head. "Not at first. Children and Family Services found me a foster home but the couple gave me back when they found out they were pregnant. After that I guess I was in and out of a couple of foster homes. I was a pretty sickly kid so I guess a lot of people didn't want to deal with that. I was finally diagnosed with a hole in my heart when I was two."

"Is that why you were never adopted?" Gray asked.

"I guess that was part of it. But I was also really quiet so when potential adoptees came around, they usually gravitated towards the active, friendly kids, not the ones who colored by themselves in the corner and refused to speak to anyone. I once heard one of the potential moms say I creeped her out."

"I'm so sorry, Luke," Gray whispered as he leaned in to brush his mouth over Luke's.

Luke shrugged. "It was the only life I knew so it wasn't so bad."

Gray doubted that but didn't point it out.

"When did you meet Rhys?"

"I was sixteen and someone at CFS must have decided I'd been in the group home long enough or they needed to make room or something because I was placed in a foster home. Rhys had already been there for a few months and for whatever reason, he decided to take me under his wing which was a good thing because a couple of the older boys started messing with me as soon as I got there. The foster dad was pretty shitty too and Rhys often took the beatings that were meant for me."

Luke pressed closer to Gray and Gray automatically wrapped his arms around him. He could feel Luke's warm breath against his throat as he spoke.

"The hole in my heart healed up when I was ten and after that I started to grow and develop more normally. I hit a growth spurt in my teens – I ended up being taller than all the other boys my age in the home and even some of the older ones so a lot of them used to call me names and make fun of me, especially since I still didn't talk much. My foster father started calling me Frankenstein and smacking me around when I didn't move fast enough to suit him – that's when Rhys would do something to provoke him so he'd go after him instead," Luke said softly. "I never would have survived that place if it hadn't been for Rhys."

"Is that why you followed him into the army?"

Luke nodded. "It was funny because all the things that had made me a freak in my childhood worked to my advantage in boot camp. I never talked back to any of my superiors and I was always focused on whatever goal they set for us. My size and strength were assets too. Not having a place to call home meant my entire focus was on my duties and not having anyone to go home to meant I didn't have the same level of fear that some of the other guys did...It was the first time I finally felt like I belonged somewhere."

"Isn't there anyone that would listen to your side of the story? A commanding officer?"

"I have no way of knowing which ones are aligned with Shaw. And since I'd be facing a court martial for Barnes' murder instead of a regular court of law, the likelihood that I'd get a fair trial is slim and the chances that Shaw would even let me live that long are slimmer."

"The press then," Gray said desperately. "They can tell your side-"

Gray's words were cut off with a kiss and when Luke pushed him onto his back, Gray got the silent message. Unlike the first night they'd been together, Gray's body responded instantly to the feel of Luke settling his weight down on him and his dick began swelling to life. He kissed Luke hungrily as he worked Luke's shirt off his chest and then he was leaning up to run his tongue over one of Luke's nipples. Luke bit out a moan at the contact but he was too desperate to slow down and he grabbed Gray's wrists and lifted them over his head so he could more easily slide Gray's shirt off of him. But to Gray's surprise, Luke pushed him back down on the bed and wrapped the shirt around his wrists. The impromptu binding wasn't tight enough that he couldn't escape but just the idea of being restrained had Gray's dick hardening to near painful proportions.

Luke sat up to enjoy his handiwork and then leaned down to seal his mouth over Gray's. The kiss left Gray humping helplessly against Luke but Luke wouldn't be rushed and Gray had to endure slow, achingly sweet kiss after kiss that only incited his need even more.

"Luke, please," he whispered against Luke's mouth.

"When you take me for the first time, I want you to do this to me" – Luke put his hands on Gray's immobilized wrists – "so all I can do is feel everything you're doing to me."

Gray sucked in a breath at that because even the idea of sliding into Luke's tight heat had his brain and his dick going into overdrive. It wasn't something they'd ever talked about and Gray was more than happy to bottom even though it wasn't something he'd done often. And the way Luke owned his body and gave back every bit of pleasure he took and then some, there was no way Gray would be able to go long without the feel of Luke filling him.

Luke's mouth crushed over his again and kissed him hungrily before he slid down Gray's body, setting his skin on fire wherever he touched it with his expert lips and greedy fingers. By the time Luke began nuzzling Gray's dick through his pants, Gray was begging incoherently for relief and even though he was able to move his bound arms, each time he did, Luke immediately stopped what he was doing so Gray left his arms exactly where they were. Any shame Gray had felt over his missing balls had disappeared after that first night when Luke had proved that Gray's body brought him pleasure exactly the way it was. So when Luke dragged his briefs off, Gray eagerly thrust his hips up in silent invitation. But to his surprise, Luke ignored his dick and turned him over and yanked him back so that he was on all fours. Cool air wafted over his hole for only a moment before Luke's, wet, hot tongue licked over him. The sensation had Gray screaming in surprise and pleasure and when Luke began both sucking and licking him, Gray dropped to his elbows and buried his face in the bedding to muffle his moans. The feel of Luke's stiff tongue breaching him had his knees threatening to give out too but Luke used his palm on Gray's stomach to offer added support.

Gray had no idea how long the blissful torture lasted but by the time Luke slid into him, Gray was just a mass of need and every part of his reality was centered in his ass where Luke's heavy cock brushed against the sensitive, smooth walls of his rectum. Luke's free hand was stroking Gray's dick which jerked every time Luke hit his prostate. Sweat dripped down Gray's face as Luke picked up the pace and by the time Luke was pounding into him, Gray had given up on trying to silence himself and between grunts and groans, he was begging Luke to let him come. When it finally happened, Gray was unprepared for the orgasm even though he'd been expecting it.

Even on the first night they'd been together, Gray hadn't expected any future orgasm he was lucky enough to have to measure up to past ones but the release Luke had coaxed from him that night had surprised him. And tonight was no different. Rolling waves of burning pleasure kept sweeping over him as Luke's heavy frame dropped onto his back. The pressure in his dick exploded and tremors of white hot pleasure ripped through every nerve ending until he could no longer feel anything but warmth surrounding him from every side. He was floating in a haze of pleasure that he would have been happy to stay in forever, especially since he could feel Luke's ragged breathing against the back of his neck. And when Luke whispered "I love you," in his ear, Gray knew for certain he was in a dream he never wanted to wake up from.

∽

"Are you sure you don't want to come with me?" Gray asked as he leaned back against the truck door and enjoyed the feel of Luke's body pressing him against the cool metal as Luke kissed the pulse point in his neck.

"No, I really want to finish the last cabinet," Luke murmured.

Gray wasn't sure if he managed a pout or not but it didn't matter because Luke sealed their mouths together and kissed him deeply before pulling Gray forward a few steps and opening the door.

"See you soon," Gray said as he climbed into the truck. "Call me if you need anything," Gray added as he glanced at the phone in Luke's pocket. The disposable cell phone was something he'd bought on impulse during his last trip to the next town over to get groceries.

"Will do," Luke said. "Why don't you take Ripley?" Luke suggested and before Gray could respond, Luke was calling the dog over and she jumped into the back seat of the truck. The big dog's entire body took up most of the back bench seat. Ripley's physical health had improved significantly since Luke had rescued her and the only proof she'd ever been abused were the scars that could be felt but not seen beneath the animal's lush coat.

Gray gave Luke a brief wave through the window and then pulled the truck onto the road that would lead down the mountain. It would only take him about thirty minutes to get to the next town over to pick up some groceries but the second Luke disappeared from his rearview mirror, Gray got the itchy feeling he'd been getting in the past couple of weeks. It made no sense since things between him and Luke had been better than ever. They hadn't spoken much about Cavelli's statements although Gray's cell phone had nearly exploded from all the calls he'd gotten from his so called friends who likely only wanted to get the "real" story so they could then leak it to the tabloids and fuel the fire that Gray refused to even acknowledge. Sid had gone apeshit when Gray had calmly told Sid he wouldn't be making a statement and he'd ended up hanging up on Sid just to shut him up.

The only tension between him and Luke had happened a couple days earlier when Gray had suggested they leave the country. He'd already been working through the details of how to charter a private jet and get past customs of a foreign country that had no extradition deal with the U.S. when Luke had adamantly shot down the idea and said no way in hell would he allow Gray to go on the run with him. Gray hadn't argued any further but that hadn't stopped him from trying to work out the holes in his plan. He had no doubt that for the right amount of money, pilots, custom agents and anyone else they needed in their escape, could be bought.

Gray hurried through the grocery store. He'd happily started wearing his ball cap and sunglasses again since his hair had finally started to grow back. He'd been so delighted just to have his eyebrows back, that he'd ended up climbing into the shower with Luke just to show him...well, not *just* to show him but it had definitely been one of the reasons he'd gotten in there. His weight was slowly starting to come back too and he felt better than he had in a long time. It was frightening how perfect his life was turning out to be – if he could just give Luke the freedom from being discovered then maybe, just maybe, they could build a life together. His gut was telling him that Luke was just as deep into the relationship as he was and since his gut had been what had brought Luke into his life in the first place, he wasn't willing to ignore it even when the little voice in his brain was saying something else.

By the time he got back to the cabin, he half-expected Luke to be waiting for him on the porch steps like he sometimes did or to at least come around the side of the cabin. But when neither happened, Gray felt a twinge of worry. He let Ripley out of the truck and trotted inside and called Luke's name. But he stopped dead when he saw the disposable cell phone sitting on the kitchen table.

He left it there by mistake, that's all.

Gray's first instinct was to go back outside and check the shed but the sight of the phone sitting on the table had him going to his bedroom instead. Luke had moved what little stuff he had into Gray's room a while back but one glance in the closet showed the duffle bag was gone. Pain lanced through Gray and he didn't bother to look in the dresser drawers to know they were empty. He also didn't waste time checking the guest bedroom – he just hurried back out of the cabin, grabbing his keys as he went.

~

A tremor went through Luke as he pulled open the door to the police station and stepped inside. Just the sight of the police cruiser sitting on the street in front of the station had had him wanting to turn around but then he remembered the desperation in Gray's voice as he explained his insane plan to go on the run with him and he strode for the door with renewed determination.

As soon as he stepped inside, Luke saw Jax sitting at one of two desks in the middle of the room. There was a reception desk right by the door but since it was empty, Luke walked past it.

"Afternoon," Jax said as his eyes took in the way Luke had purposefully held his arms out from his body, his palms open, the strap of his duffle bag hanging from one hand.

"I'm here to turn myself in," Luke said quietly as he carefully lowered the bag to the floor. He wasn't surprised when the deputy stiffened at his statement and then stood and came around his desk. "I'm not armed but I have an unloaded gun and ammunition in my bag. You'll find a warrant out for my arrest out of Fort Benning in Georgia. Luke Monroe. M.O.N-"

"Luke?"

Luke turned his head at the sound of the familiar voice. The sight of his stunned foster brother would have been amusing if Luke's mind wasn't so preoccupied with other things. Like the hell he was about to face. And the betrayal Gray would feel when he found out what Luke had done.

"It's me, Rhys," Luke said tiredly.

Rhys' green eyes went wider and then a huge smile split his face and he was striding across the small space and dragging Luke into his arms. He'd apparently failed to notice Jax's tense frame or heard Luke's reason for being there.

"What the hell are you doing here?" Rhys asked as he still held on to him and Luke felt a pang of longing go through him. This man had been such an important part of his life and he'd been foolish enough to let that go. And now he'd have to watch the light go out in Rhys' eyes as he realized the kid he'd sacrificed so much for was now a man he'd have to arrest.

Rhys put space between them and then scanned Luke up and down. "You look really good," he announced before giving Luke another hug.

It was on the tip of Luke's tongue to tell Rhys the same thing because the man looked happier than Luke had even thought possible – well, at least before he'd met Gray and learned what it was that could put that look on a man's face. His thought was interrupted by the door behind him being yanked open and he knew before he even turned around who it was. When he did force himself to turn, his heart fell at the shocked look in Gray's face. It was clear that while Gray had discovered he was gone, he hadn't expected to find him there at the police station.

"No," Gray whispered as he glanced from Luke to Jax. He shook his head violently. "No!" But then his eyes turned to Jax. "Jax, please don't do this. I'm begging you!"

The heartbreak in Gray's voice had Luke pulling free of the light hold Rhys still had on him and he went to stand in front of Gray. He grabbed hold of Gray's arm and said, "Gray, Jax didn't arrest me. I came here to turn myself in."

His statement caught Gray off guard and though Luke wouldn't have thought it possible, the pain in his gaze intensified. "Why?"

"You know why," Luke said.

Gray shook his head again and then he was throwing his arms around Luke. "Don't say anything, okay? My lawyer can be here in a few hours. I'll get you the best defense money can buy-" Gray stammered.

A sense of cold washed through Luke as he realized what Gray was saying was completely true. The man would move heaven and earth to save him. He'd spend every day of his life and every dollar in his bank account to try to keep Luke out of jail only to die a slow death as he watched the man he loved rot in prison...and that was only by some twist of fate that kept Shaw from getting to him first. Desperation went through Luke as he glanced from Gray to Jax and then Rhys. He could tell Jax knew what he was about to do and the man actually looked like he was shaking his head. But Luke ignored him and turned his attention back to Gray.

"Gray, go home," he said firmly and he forced himself to release his lover.

"No," Gray snapped as he pulled his cell phone from his pocket and began dialing. Luke grabbed it from him and tossed it on a nearby desk.

"Gray, listen to me," Luke said.

"No," Gray nearly yelled as he tried to grab the phone.

"Damn it, Gray, haven't you figured it out yet? I don't want you!" he shouted.

The words had the desired effect and Gray stepped back as if Luke had struck him. But then his eyes hardened and Luke knew it wasn't going to be that easy so he went in for the kill. "Even if by some miracle your lawyer sorts all this shit out, do you really think I'd stay here with you? After everything I told you about the military being my life?"

Gray paled but thankfully didn't say anything. Not that it would have mattered because Luke felt like he had a mortal wound inside of him tearing open. "Did you think I'd actually want to be walking down some red carpet by your side, smiling for the cameras like some trained monkey all the while wondering what actor or groupie you were fucking behind my back?" Luke gave the knife one last twist by whispering, "You needed someone to take care of you, Gray, and I needed a place to hide out. The stuff between us was just a ...perk."

Luke actually had to grab the desk to keep himself upright at that point but Gray's response was the exact opposite. His pretty gold eyes dimmed and then they went blank and Luke knew in that instant that his Gray was gone. The man before him merely reached past him to grab the cell phone off the desk and then he turned and walked out the door. He heard Gray's truck start up a second later but there wasn't even the squeal of tires to accompany the sound – no, his lie had done exactly what he'd intended. He turned his attention to Jax and ground out, "Luke Monroe. M.O.N.R.O.E. The charge is murder in the first degree."

~

"Tell me what's going on," Luke heard Rhys say softly as a cup of coffee was pushed into his lax grip. The windowless room they were sitting in felt too small but he supposed it was better than a jail cell. He also wasn't cuffed yet so there was that too. Not that it mattered because he'd been frozen within himself for the last ten minutes and didn't even remember how he'd made it to the room with the small wood table and chairs.

"I should probably get an attorney first," Luke whispered because that was the best he could manage considering his throat actually hurt.

"Fuck that," Rhys snapped and then he was up and pacing the small room. It was so *Rhys*. Even when they were kids, Rhys had never been able to hide his feelings or sit still when confronted with something beyond his control. And he almost never accepted the fact that he couldn't jump in and save someone or fix the situation.

"You can tell the sheriff that I'm waiving my right to an extradition hearing-"

Rhys slammed his hand down on the table. Lesser men would have jumped at the abrupt move but Luke merely used his sleeve to dab at the splash of coffee that that had sloshed over the cup and onto the table.

"Murder charges? What the hell happened?" Rhys bit out.

Luke sighed and then rehashed the story for Rhys. Rhys didn't interrupt him at all but as soon as he was done he was asking question after question, just like any good cop would. Since his heart still felt like it had been run through by a knife, Luke finally cut Rhys off and said, "Make the call, Rhys. You know you don't have a choice."

"Fuck if I don't," Rhys snapped but he finally sat down. "Why didn't you come to me when you got here?"

"Because I knew you'd go through hell and high water to help me even if meant giving this up," Luke said as he waved his hand at Rhys' uniform.

"So your plan was to leave? Just like that? Without even talking to me?"

"That was the plan," Luke acknowledged.

"And then you met Gray?"

Even the sound of Gray's name had Luke nearly keeling over in pain so he just nodded.

"Did...did something happen between you two?" Rhys asked, his voice gentle.

Luke could feel tears threatening and he had to blink his eyes rapidly to stop them from falling. "I felt something that first day... something I'd never felt for another man."

"You were attracted to him?" Rhys offered.

Luke nodded. "But it was so much more than that. I was confused by the physical part of it but it was also the little stuff, you know?" Luke asked, though one look at Rhys told him the man wasn't sure what he was talking about.

"Like the sound of his laugh or the way his smile is a little higher on one side of his mouth than the other or the way he would sneak Ripley food from his plate when he didn't think I was watching." Luke shook his head in frustration because even as he spoke, he realized that the words didn't do justice for how he felt around Gray.

"Being around him is what I always thought coming home would feel like...but the kind of coming home you and I never got to have when we were kids, you know?"

A smile spread across Rhys' features making him look much younger than his 30 years. "I do know," he said wistfully and Luke could only imagine that the man was thinking about his lovers. Gray hadn't been able to tell Luke much about the two men Rhys had become involved with after his arrival in Dare but it was clear that whatever was happening between the three of them, it was exactly what Rhys needed.

"The things you said to him..." Rhys said, his features darkening.

Luke buried his face in his hands. "He wanted to give up his whole life just so he could go on the run with me."

"And that's why you turned yourself in?"

"What could I offer him, Rhys? Looking over his shoulder for the rest of his life? Never being able to contact his friends or family again? Always terrified he'd make a mistake that would get me or himself caught? You saw him out there – he wasn't going to let me go! The man just spent the last two months fighting for his life and I'm supposed to ask him to sit around and wait for me in the hopes that I one day get out of prison? Or to waste his life savings on a defense that won't do a bit of good? Or panic every time the phone rings because he knows it could be the call that says Shaw finally finished what he started?"

Rhys was quiet for a long time before he said, "From what I saw out there, he's already in as deep as he can be, whether you want him to be or not. He's not some foster family that's going to dump you when things get to complicated, Luke."

Before Luke could answer, there was a rap on the door and then Jax was pushing it open, his phone in hand. "I think we might have a problem," he murmured as he held the phone out to Rhys. "Dane just texted it to me. He saw it on the Internet a few minutes ago."

Rhys glanced at the phone and then bit out a curse before handing the phone to Luke. Fear went through Luke as he saw the picture of him and Gray sitting on the porch steps leading up to Gray's cabin. He knew right away that the image had been snapped two days before when he and Gray had decided to sit outside after dinner and have a cup of coffee while they watched the sun set. While his name wasn't mentioned, his image was clear as day.

"Jesus," he muttered and he quickly clicked off the image to find the article. He bypassed the title and found what he was looking for. "Oh God, this has been online since yesterday morning," he whispered. "I need to warn Gray," he said as he stood and started looking for the contact list on Jax's phone.

Jax took the phone from him and began scrolling but when a landline phone in the other room rang, he handed his cell to Rhys and left the room. Rhys found the number and hit dial but didn't hand the phone to Luke. "He may not talk to you," was all Rhys said in way of explanation. "Straight to voicemail," Rhys muttered a moment later.

"We have a problem," Jax announced as he strode back into the room. To Luke's surprise, the man leaned down and grabbed a revolver from his ankle holster and handed it to Luke.

"911 just got a call from a guy claiming to be a reporter. He says he's across the road from Gray's place and he just heard a gunshot go off."

Luke was moving before Jax even finished talking. He reached the sidewalk and began looking for a car to boost but then a hand settled on his arm. "You and Rhys take my car and I'll follow you," Jax said as he tossed some car keys to Rhys. Luke followed Rhys to a black SUV while Jax ran to the patrol car sitting in front of the station.

Terror sparked through Luke even as he tried to call up the coolness he would need to confront Shaw because he had no doubt in his mind that the man had finally found him and because of his stupidity, Gray was caught in the crosshairs.

CHAPTER 10

*G*ray barely had time to spit out the mouthful of blood before the fist slammed into his face again. This time, the blow caught him along the cheek and he felt hot liquid running down the side of his face and then down his neck a second later.

The time from when he'd left the station and had arrived back at the cabin had been a complete blur except for the brief call he'd put in to his lawyer to tell him to catch the next flight to Montana. He hadn't given the man any details other than to meet Luke at the Dare Police Department and to spare no expense in preparing the man's defense. He had no memory of the drive after that because he'd been too numb to feel anything. His only thought had been to stop at home long enough to pack a bag so as soon as he'd pulled the truck to a stop in the driveway, he'd let Ripley out of the backseat and then hurried to the cabin. The dog had disappeared around back somewhere and Gray hadn't bothered to call her back since the animal would need as much time as possible to stretch her legs before Gray got her back in the car and pointed his truck south. His goal had been to put as many miles between himself and Luke as possible. He'd been so distracted that he hadn't even noticed that the cabin door was unlocked and he'd already been halfway to the kitchen before he realized he wasn't alone.

He'd stopped dead at the sight of a man in military garb standing near the kitchen table pointing a gun at him but it was when another spoke up from behind him that he'd turned around and realized he was staring at the same man who'd tried to take Luke's life not once, but twice. The man was as clean cut as they came and held himself with an air of confidence that bordered on swagger. His dark eyes had sized Gray up quickly and Gray had actually felt a shiver go through him at the cool dismissal. And in that moment, Gray had known he would be used as a tool and nothing more. So when Shaw had barked at him to tell him where Luke was, Gray had said the words he'd spent a lifetime perfecting.

Fuck off.

As he waffled between awareness and the promise of an imminent blackout, Gray could hear Ripley going crazy outside as she had been for the past ten minutes. From the dog's wild barking, he could tell the animal was running back and forth between the front and back of the cabin in a vain effort to find a way inside. At first, Shaw had seemed amused when the dog's huge face and paws would appear in the window by the kitchen as the other man worked Gray over, but at some point he'd gotten annoyed because he fired several times at the dog through the glass. Ripley's incessant barking was the only evidence that the man had missed but Gray was terrified that it would only be a matter of time. And every time the man who Shaw had referred to only as Quincy had hit him, Ripley's outcry only became more agitated.

While the first several punches had hurt like hell, a warmth had settled in Gray's limbs after a while and he no longer felt the same level of pain as each blow fell. One of his eyes was swollen shut but he could still hear well enough and he took a perverse pleasure in the sound of Shaw's growing frustration as Gray remained silent every time he asked where Luke was. From the beating he was taking, Gray knew either Shaw would soon tire of asking the same question or he'd realize Gray's answer wasn't going to differ from his original one and he'd take a bullet to the brain. Gray almost wanted to laugh at the irony of it all because Luke was finally in the safest place he could be even though he doubted that had been Luke's intent when he'd gone to the station.

"Fucker must have a nice dick to earn himself this kind of loyalty," he heard Shaw mutter in his ear. "Or does that faggot like taking it instead?"

Gray only managed to say "Fuck-" before a fist slammed into his face again and he had no doubt that his nose was broken because blood poured down into his already blood-filled mouth.

"We're wasting our time here," Shaw snapped as he straightened. "Finish it. Let's leave our friend a message he won't soon forget," he added.

Gray moaned as a hand reached from behind him and yanked his head back to expose his throat. It wasn't until he saw the flash of a knife that he realized Shaw wasn't going to waste a bullet on him. He closed his good eye and searched his mind for an image of Luke and a ripple of pleasure went through him as he realized how many he had to choose from – Luke smiling at something on TV, Luke playing tug of war over a stick with Ripley, Luke's lips hovering over his as Luke slipped into his body.

A feeling of peace settled over him as he drew what he assumed would be his last breath but the kiss of the knife never came because all of a sudden there was the sound of glass shattering behind him and he was thrown forward. With his hands tied behind his back and his ankles bound to the chair he was sitting in, Gray had no way to brace himself and he hit the ground hard but managed to stay conscious. He could hear a man swearing and the sound of Ripley snarling. Gray managed to turn himself enough to see Ripley had somehow managed to break through the bullet riddled window and had the guy with the knife on the floor and was biting him on the arm. The man's struggles did nothing to dislodge the pissed off dog but it didn't matter because Ripley suddenly howled in pain as a gunshot rang out and then fell to the floor.

"No!" Gray shouted as he tried to break free of the bindings.

"Fuck, my arm!" Quincy shouted as he struggled to his feet, blood pouring from his arm where both the sleeve and his skin were completely shredded.

"Shut up!" Shaw yelled. A second later he said, "He's here – cover the back in case he's not alone. Now!"

Quincy pulled his gun free from the holster at his side and he went towards the back of the cabin. Gray could only assume he was going towards the door that led into the backyard just off the small mud room.

An arm wrapped around Gray's throat and dragged him up until the chair was upright once more. He felt the cold metal of a gun pressed to his head just as the front door slowly swung open.

"It's me, Shaw."

Gray's denial at the sound of Luke's voice got lost in his throat as he watched Luke step unarmed into the cabin.

∼

It took every ounce of Luke's training not to react at the sight of Gray. Between the blood streaming out of Gray's nose and mouth, his blackened left eye that was swollen completely shut and the gun pressed to his temple, Luke was nearly overcome with his need to stride up to Shaw and beat him within an inch of his life just before he snapped his neck and relished the cracking sound.

"Lift your shirt and turn around," Shaw brusquely ordered and Luke reined in his temper and did as he was told. He ignored Gray's look of fear as he also slowly lifted the hem of each of his pant legs to show he wasn't hiding a weapon there. While Shaw visibly relaxed when he confirmed Luke wasn't carrying a gun, he kept his aimed at Gray's head and Luke knew even the slightest twitch of Shaw's finger could cause the gun to go off.

"What, no pleas to let him go now that you're here?" Shaw sniped.

"Did begging do that mother any good before you slaughtered her kids?" Luke asked coldly. "Did Barnes beg you not to blow his brains out?"

131

Shaw laughed and the sound grated against Luke's ears.

"Bastard didn't even see it coming. Not a sharp one, that guy," Shaw said.

"You trusted him enough to do your dirty work," Luke responded.

Shaw laughed again. "If that were true, you'd be six feet under in a pine box, not him. Fucker was supposed to take care of you in the hospital – his penance for not being able to pull the trigger in that shithole."

The news surprised Luke since he'd just assumed it was Barnes who had shot him.

"You should have seen how relieved he was when he told me you didn't remember anything and probably never would – little fucker and his hero worship." Shaw's bitter tone drifted off as he suddenly began massaging the barrel of the gun back and forth against Gray's temple, almost as if it were a caress.

"Now that I know you have a penchant for cock instead of pussy, makes me wonder if there wasn't something else going on between the two of you."

When Shaw pressed his gun into the open wound on Gray's cheek, Luke saw Gray try to hold back his cry of pain but Shaw seemed unsatisfied with the lack of reaction and jammed his gun hard against the bloody injury. Gray moaned and closed his good eye.

"I was gone, Shaw. You won! Why the fuck did you come after me?" Luke yelled. His outburst got Shaw's attention back on him enough so that the gun was no longer digging into Gray's wound.

"You disrespectful son of a bitch – always thinking you were smarter than me. Always so high and mighty knowing the men looked to you for approval after I gave the order. You really think I'm stupid enough to think you wouldn't try to screw me out of my future? The future I earned?"

Luke stared at the narcissistic son of a bitch in disbelief. "Is that what you call killing three little kids and an innocent woman? You're a fucking murderer, Shaw. You didn't earn anything! And what about Eddie?"

Shaw waved his gun briefly. "A casualty of war, just like that woman and her brats. You think this country will fault me for what happened? They ought to give me a fucking medal! How many lives did I save by eliminating three future terrorists? And that woman – what was to stop her from strapping on a suicide vest and walking up to our men pretending to be a friendly, huh?"

The man was fucking insane and that fact had Luke's fear ratcheting up a notch. The mental count he had going on in his head was nearing its end so he focused his gaze on Gray. But the man's one good eye was still closed and Luke wanted to shout in frustration because he had only seconds left. Luke heard the tell-tale pop he'd been waiting for and a second later Gray finally opened his eye. They locked gazes and then Luke quickly glanced at the ground before looking back up at Gray. He did the gesture again for good measure just as there was a commotion behind the cabin. A man's hoarse shout was cut short and the second Shaw glanced behind him to see what had caused the sound, Gray threw all his weight to his left and he and the chair crashed to the floor. Luke launched himself at Shaw and grunted as he felt a sharp pain in his arm. Shaw was already pulling the trigger again when Luke's weight hit him and the next bullet flew past Luke's ear. He managed to get Shaw on his stomach and wrapped an arm around his neck as yet another gunshot rang out but then an image of Gray's terrified, battered face flashed through his mind and he did exactly what he'd been wanting to do and snapped Shaw's neck like it was a dry, rotted piece of wood.

∾

"Luke, there's a guy out here who says he's Gray's brother," Rhys said from the doorway of Gray's hospital room.

"Let him in," Luke said as he glanced at Gray to see if Rhys' voice had woken him up. Satisfied that Gray was still asleep, Luke settled back in his chair next to the bed. Roman was slow to enter the room and Luke guessed it was because he was struggling to take in his brother's appearance.

After Luke had killed Shaw, he'd scrambled to Gray's side only to find that Gray had struck his head on the floor hard enough to knock himself out. He'd woken up in the ambulance but he'd been confused and in a lot of pain so the ER doctor had given him a heavy dose of painkillers as well as a sedative. He'd been out ever since and Luke had been left to stare at his lover's broken body as the guilt of knowing he was the cause of everything that had happened to the man he loved gnawed at him. And he'd ended up hurting Gray for nothing because Shaw had still gotten to him.

Roman's dark blue gaze met his across the bed as he moved closer to his brother and Luke wasn't surprised to see the fury in them. He just wasn't sure if it was directed at him or not.

"Is he..."

"He's sleeping," Luke said softly. "The doctor gave him a sedative so he'll be out for a little while but he's going to be okay."

Roman's eyes stayed on Gray as he spoke. "I went by the cabin and they told me what happened."

"He said you were going to try to stop by on your way back to L.A."

Roman nodded. "I saw the picture of you and him on the Internet. I didn't want him to think I told anyone..."

"We know it wasn't you who told the press where he was, Roman. I'll make sure he knows that."

"The man who did this..."

"Dead."

"He was someone you knew?"

"Yes. Gray's here because of me...because of my past."

Roman's emotion filled gaze lifted to meet his. He hadn't gotten much of a sense about the other man the first time they'd met but he definitely didn't seem as detached as Gray seemed to think he was.

"You love him?" Roman asked.

"Very much."

Roman merely nodded and then his dark eyes shifted back to Gray. "And the cancer..."

"Gone for now. He'll have to get tested several times over the next year and then regularly after that but the doctor is hopeful he'll stay in remission."

"And if he doesn't?"

Luke heard the unasked question and knew in that instant that whatever had happened between the two brothers, it wasn't unfixable. It would just probably fall on Gray to make the first move.

"I'll be there. Always."

Roman seemed satisfied with the response and actually leaned down to put his hand over Gray's. But the contact was brief and then he was stepping back.

"You should stay a while, Roman," Luke suggested though he could tell by the tension in the man's frame that he was already mentally out the door.

"I have some business back home," Roman said quietly.

"Is there anything you want me to tell him?" Luke asked.

Roman studied Gray for a long time before finally saying, "Tell him thanks for the nightlight."

~

*G*ray hurt all over but it was a dull, hollow pain that was hidden just under a cloud of something warm and pleasant. Part of him wanted to just keep his eyes closed and enjoy the curious sensation but then images began flashing in his mind and he couldn't tell if they were real or some terrible nightmare. He jerked upright but didn't make it very far because a warm hand settled on his shoulder and held him down.

"Gray, it's okay. You're safe."

He'd know that voice anywhere. Gray managed to pry his eyes open, though it took him several tries. But when he tried to speak, no sound came out. A straw was pressed against his lips and he took a few swallows of water that cooled his parched throat. As he drank, his eyes shifted to his right and a sigh of relief went through him when he saw that Luke appeared to be unharmed.

"He shot you," Gray managed to croak.

"The bullet just grazed me...again," Luke said and when he sat down in the chair that was sitting next to the bed, he pulled up his sleeve and showed Gray a bandage covering his bicep. Relief went through Gray but then another memory assaulted him.

"Ripley...oh God, Luke, she jumped through the window..."

"She's okay, Gray. Jax got her to Dane in time. She needed surgery and a transfusion but Dane says she'll make it."

"What happened to Shaw? How...How did you know he was at the cabin?"

Gray automatically pulled his hand free as Luke's fingers covered his, because along with all the terrible memories of Shaw's assault came the painful words that had sent him running back to the cabin. Luke's words.

Luke's face fell at Gray's withdrawal but he said, "A paparazzo that was hiding out in the trees across the road from your cabin called 911 when he heard the gunshots. He had a high powered lens on his camera so he was able to get some pictures of us together a couple days ago."

"That's how Shaw found you," Gray breathed.

"Dane saw the picture on the Internet and called Jax. We were getting ready to come out to the cabin when the 911 call came in about shots fired at your place. Jax questioned the reporter afterwards. He said your agent, Sid, was the one who told him where you were, Gray," Luke said softly. "Sid admitted that he got the information from the lawyer who handled the trust you used to buy the property. I guess they were friends."

"Any publicity is good publicity," Gray murmured. "Probably Sid's way of trying to force me into making a statement about Cavelli."

"Fucker nearly cost you your life," Luke growled.

Under any other circumstance, Luke's protectiveness would have caused a warm shiver to run up his spine but now it just frustrated him. "How did you get Shaw?"

"Jax used a high powered rifle to distract the guy guarding the back door. The sound drew him out enough for Rhys to take him out and that distracted Shaw enough for me to get to him. He's dead."

Gray nodded and he hated the rush of relief that went through him knowing Luke was free now. Free to go back to the life he loved.

"Your lawyer showed up at the police station a couple hours ago. Said he was my lawyer, actually."

Gray turned on his side so he wouldn't have to face Luke anymore because whatever drug was coursing through his blood was doing nothing to ease the ache in his heart. "I'm really tired, Luke. Thanks for stopping by."

Gray heard movement behind him and his whole body drew tight as he sensed Luke leaning over him. Lips ghosted across his forehead and then stopped by his ear. "Don't think this is goodbye, Gray, because I'm not going anywhere."

CHAPTER 11

Three weeks. Three fucking weeks.

That was how long it had taken Luke to clear up the shitstorm that had rained down on him when word got out of Shaw's actions overseas and at home. But it hadn't even started there. It had started after what should have been a simple run to the cafeteria to get a cup of coffee while Gray was asleep. By the time he'd gotten back to Gray's room, a burly security guard had been waiting by the door and a grim looking Rhys had informed him that Gray had said he didn't want to see him anymore. He'd fought it of course but no amount of calling Gray's name had changed anything and he hadn't been willing to hurt Rhys just to get past him. So he'd finally allowed Rhys to escort him from the hospital where his foster brother had dropped another load of bad news on him – until the mess with Barnes' murder was cleared up, Luke was technically under arrest. And while Rhys hadn't gone so far as to cuff him, he had taken him back to the station where two MPs had been waiting for him to escort him back to Fort Benning. Rhys, as well as the lawyer Gray had hired for him, had followed and Luke was actually grateful for the attorney's presence because he'd been too overcome with anguish to care about the legal crap going on around him. While Gray's attorney had worked to secure his freedom, Luke had been trying to figure out how to get Gray back.

Three weeks later and he wasn't much closer to his goal. He'd managed to convince Dane to give him Gray's address in California after he discovered that Gray had left Montana a couple days after he'd been discharged from the hospital. He hadn't bothered trying to call Gray because he knew Gray would tell him to go to hell, and the things he needed to say couldn't be done over the phone. And although he hadn't seen or spoken to Gray in person, he had seen his former lover in all his glory as he became exactly what he he'd been so afraid of – a role model.

The first interview had been on some type of nightly entertainment show about a week after Shaw's assault. Luke had taken in every detail of Gray's still bruised face and he'd listened as Gray had glossed over his injuries and the details of what had happened that day. And before the reporter could ask her next question, Gray had stunned her and likely the entire audience with his announcement that he had been battling cancer. The reporter had recovered quickly to ask endless and increasingly personal questions and Gray had answered every single one openly and honestly and as the interview drew to a close, he'd looked straight at the camera and sent a message directly to the audience asking them not to wait to go to the doctor if they found anything suspicious. He'd also encouraged anyone battling the disease to find a support system among their family and friends so they would have the strength they needed to become a survivor instead of a statistic. More interviews and articles had followed as Gray became the face of surviving testicular cancer and if the new label bothered him at all, he never showed it.

But it was what Luke hadn't seen that had him buying a one-way ticket to L.A. instead of driving and then paying a cab driver an exorbitant fee to get him out of the crowded city and on the way to the posh beachside community of Malibu. All the words coming out of Gray's mouth had been the right ones but there'd been nothing in his eyes. When he'd told the reporter he was excited to be working with the studio on the final version of the script for the first film in his series, there'd been no excitement in his golden eyes. The wide smile that accompanied the reporter's congratulations on his latest book making the bestseller list a month before its release date was too wide. And when asked about the mysterious man Gray had been with at his cabin, Gray couldn't mask the pain in his eyes even as he coyly dodged the question.

Finding Gray's house was surprisingly easy because there were at least half a dozen reporters standing at the edge of the driveway. Luke was glad there wasn't any kind of security gate to get through and he ignored the reporters calling out to him when he got out of the cab. He'd packed light for the trip so he didn't need to spend any time digging luggage from the cab's trunk. But it was an odd feeling to have cameras and flashes going off behind him as he made his way up the walkway of the very modern looking white house. His anxiety was at boiling point and it seemed to take forever for the door to open. But nothing could have prepared him for his first sight of Gray.

It wasn't that there was anything outwardly wrong with Gray's physical appearance - in fact, he actually looked healthier than Luke had ever seen him. His beautiful blond hair was almost back to the length it had been that terrible day when he'd watched Gray shave the first of it off and his skin no longer looked pale or sallow. And while he was still a little underweight, his body had started to fill out enough that his clothes fit normally again. But what Luke was seeing was only a shell of a man. There was no spark in his dull eyes and even upon seeing Luke, his expression barely changed.

"Hi," was all Luke managed to come up with as his hungry eyes raked over Gray. Gray didn't say anything but he did open the door wider and Luke took that as the only invitation he was going to get. As soon as he was inside, Ripley came up to greet him. The dog's movements were slow and she had a slight limp but her tail was wagging and she whined excitedly as she pressed her nose into Luke's hand.

"She looks good," Luke murmured as he got on the smooth white floor and let Ripley crawl all over him. He used the time to take in the inside of Gray's house and was overwhelmed by how beautiful it was…and expensive looking. Huge glass windows made up the entire rear, giving him an unfettered view of the beach and ocean. The living room boasted a massive fireplace and had several pieces of leather furniture positioned in a way that guests could talk to each other while still enjoying the view. A marble staircase led to the second floor and off to the side of the house he could see an indoor swimming pool.

"What are you doing here, Luke?" Gray asked tiredly as he began walking up the stairs. Luke gently extricated himself from Ripley and climbed to his feet. The big dog trotted into the living room and curled up in a plush dog bed by the fireplace.

Luke followed Gray upstairs to what he could only assume was the master bedroom. The king sized bed actually looked small in the large room, and the far wall was another set of windows. But there was also a walk out porch with a hot tub. What stood out to Luke though, were the stacked boxes stuffed into each corner of the room.

"Are you moving?" Luke asked as Gray disappeared into the closet. He returned a moment later with a large suitcase which he put on the bed and opened.

"I'm going back to the cabin."

"Are you selling this place?"

Gray merely nodded.

"What about your career? The movies?"

"I can write from anywhere," Gray murmured as he went back to the closet and reemerged with an armful of clothes.

"And the movies?"

"I told the studio I wasn't interested in being involved in the creative process. They can cast whoever they want – my only obligation is to do some promotion work when each film is released."

"So that fucker Cavelli is going to get the part even after the shit he pulled?"

Gray finally seemed to wake up from whatever haze he was in and all the emotion that had been missing from his features during all his interviews came flooding back at once. "Damn it, Luke, what the hell do you want from me?"

At the naked pain in Gray's voice, Luke cursed himself for getting off track and he tried reaching for Gray. But Gray shrugged him off and took several steps back.

"I didn't mean those things I said at the police station," Luke said softly.

Gray surprised him by saying, "I know."

Hope flared to life in Luke's chest and he closed the distance between them but Gray held out his hand to stop him and his whole body appeared to curl in on itself like it was trying to protect itself from Luke's touch. The sight had bile rising up in Luke's throat. "Gray..." he whispered in confusion.

"I know you said those things to drive me away. I get that," Gray said hoarsely. "But they're in my head now – they're all I fucking hear," his face crumpled and tears began falling from his eyes.

Luke stepped back as shockwaves went through him. God, what the hell had he done? He hadn't just wounded Gray – he'd fucking torn him apart. Horror slammed into him as he realized that while Gray had recovered from the brutal beating Shaw had inflicted on him, he was still hemorrhaging from the wounds that Luke's cruel, careless words had left behind.

"Gray, tell me how to fix this," he pleaded desperately.

Gray just shook his head and wiped at his face with his sleeve. "Can't," was all he said.

Cold settled into Luke's chest and he began to feel lightheaded so he sat down on Gray's bed. "I thought...I thought I was doing the right thing. I really did, Gray," he whispered as he looked up to search out the other man's eyes. But Gray's head was turned away and Luke knew his presence was only hurting him more. He'd lost him. He'd fucking lost Gray...and all because he'd been too scared to let the only person besides Rhys who ever truly loved him all the way in.

Luke forced himself to stand even though his legs felt like they were going to give out any minute. "Um, your brother stopped by the hospital...he wanted me to tell you 'thanks for the nightlight.' I hope you know what that means because he didn't stick around long enough to explain."

Luke turned to go but stopped when he heard Gray say, "It was the first night he came to live with us. He came into my room crying because he was afraid his mom wouldn't be able to find him from heaven. I gave him my nightlight and told him it would help her find her way so she could watch over him."

Another wave of agony tore through Luke as he said, "Don't let him push you away, Gray."

With those words, Luke's voice finally broke and he barely managed to whisper, "I love you, Gray" before he hurried from the room, tears flooding his vision. He thought he heard his name being called but he didn't have the courage to turn around and find out in case it wasn't true, so he rushed down the stairs and yanked the door open. Something hit him from behind, forcing the door shut and Luke lost it as he felt Gray's solid body pressed up against his back. Sobs racked his body as gentle hands turned him around and he went willing into Gray's arms when they wrapped around him.

~

Relief flooded Gray's entire system as Luke clung to him. In the split second he'd watched Luke leave his room, Gray had relived every moment they'd had together and while the hurt from Luke's words in the police station was still there, the joy and peace Luke had brought him were stronger and he knew that letting Luke go wasn't an option.

"Gray, I love you so much," Luke whispered against his neck. Gray could feel hot tears soaking through his shirt but he wasn't a hundred percent sure they were just Luke's. "I never wanted to hurt you..."

"I know, baby," Gray murmured against Luke's ear before pressing a gentle kiss to his head. "We'll figure it out. Just...just don't leave me again, okay?"

He thought he heard Luke whisper "never" against his neck but he wasn't sure. When Luke's sobs slowed, Gray linked their hands and led him back up the stairs. He pushed the suitcase to the floor, sat Luke down on the bed and worked his shoes off. Gray crawled over

Luke and lay down on the bed, holding his hand out. Luke took it instantly, settling down next to him, putting his head on Gray's chest. The arms that wrapped around Gray were like steel bands but Gray didn't protest the tight hold – he relished it.

They lay like that for a while and Gray didn't even realize they'd fallen asleep until he woke up and saw that it was dark outside. Luke stirred against him and when his lax grip tightened, Gray knew he was awake.

"What happened in Georgia?" he asked.

"Lots of legal shit and red tape and then endless debriefings. I lost track after a while because it seemed like all I was doing was answering the same questions over and over."

"They dropped the charges?"

Luke nodded. "I should have listened to you, Gray. About the lawyer, about asking Rhys and Jax for help – all of it."

"It all worked out," Gray murmured.

He was surprised when Luke suddenly shifted his weight so that he was hovering over him. "Don't do that," Luke said softly. "Don't let me off like it was nothing." Luke's fingers came up to trace the scar on his face.

"I wanted you to trust me," Gray finally admitted. "I wanted to give you what you gave me."

"You did," Luke whispered and then he was reaching across Gray to turn the light on the nightstand on. He reached into his pocket and pulled out a wad of folded up pages. "I had to fill out a ton of forms for the hearings, my discharge papers, the debriefings...but I didn't actually notice what I'd been doing until I filled out the paperwork for the storage place where I left my stuff after I moved it out of base housing."

Luke flattened out all the papers and handed them to Gray. Gray wasn't sure what he was looking for and was about to ask when he finally saw it. His name. It was written in the *Next of Kin/Emergency Contact* section. He sucked in a breath when he flipped to the next page and saw the same thing. Every single page had his name on it instead of the fake name Luke had used for the mother who didn't exist.

"I finally have someone who cares if I come home or not," Luke whispered against his lips.

"Always," Gray said just before Luke's mouth closed over his.

~

One kiss – one soft kiss was all it had taken to set their bodies ablaze with need but when Gray palmed Luke's ass to force their cocks together, Luke rolled them so he was on his back and Gray was settled between his legs.

"I need you inside me," Luke said as his hands framed Gray's face.

"Are you sure?" Gray asked.

Luke nodded as he yanked his shirt over his head.

"Can the restraints wait till next time?" Gray asked with a small smile.

Luke laughed as he remembered his request to have Gray tie him up the first time he made love to Luke.

"I'll still make sure you feel everything I'm going to do to you," Gray promised huskily as he nipped at Luke's lips while they worked the rest of their clothes off.

"Next time," Luke conceded and then he closed his eyes and let out a moan as Gray's tongue latched on to one of his nipples. Gray tortured the other before moving lower and searching out Luke's belly button. But instead of stopping to give some love to his swollen dick, Gray continued down his legs and even to his feet before slowly making his way up his body again. And the man never once touched his raging hard-on.

"Gray," Luke grumbled.

Gray silenced him with an almost brutal kiss that left him breathless and all of Gray's playfulness disappeared as his next pass down Luke's body was a carnal assault on his senses. Fingers, lips, tongue, teeth – they touched him everywhere, sometimes gentle, sometimes bordering on just this side of pain. But each contact just drove his need higher and higher and when Gray's mouth did finally suck him in deep, the shock of it had Luke screaming in relief as he began shooting down Gray's throat. The orgasm completely consumed him and when it was over, the only things he could move were his lips when Gray kissed him. Drops of come transferred from Gray's mouth to his and Luke shivered as his own bitter, salty essence slid down his throat. He felt Gray settle all of his weight on top of him as he peppered his face with gentle kisses and when Luke finally opened his eyes, Gray's were right there to welcome him.

"Missed you so much," Luke managed to get out despite the well of emotion in his throat. He'd come too close to losing this...way too close.

"I love you, Luke. No matter what happens, please don't ever doubt that. Only you," Gray said almost desperately.

"Never again, Gray," Luke said.

Gray nodded and then kissed him. The seduction began all over again and by the time Gray's mouth reached Luke's cock, it was once again at full attention. But instead of sucking him deep, Gray just licked him a few times and then his mouth went lower. Although he had mentally prepared himself for this moment, Luke realized the second Gray's tongue flicked over his hole that all his mental preparation had been for shit.

"Fuck, yes!" Luke cried out as Gray caressed him over and over. Each lick had pre-come dripping from Luke's cock and he couldn't resist closing his hand over the hot flesh and stroking it to match Gray's touch. The feeling of Gray's stiff tongue pushing into him had Luke freezing completely as he tried to adjust to the sensation of the intimate caress but after just one lick, Luke was frantically jerking at his dick while he pressed his ass against Gray's talented mouth. He muttered a colorful protest when Gray's tongue slipped from his body and moved upwards but then Gray was licking over his balls and Luke released his dick so he could push himself up with his hands to watch. The sight of Gray between his legs, drawing Luke's testicles into his mouth and sucking on them proved to be too much and Luke dropped back on the bed and put an arm over his eyes. He barely noticed when Gray released him because his body was so sensitive that wherever Gray's skin touched his, he felt sparks of electricity dancing around.

"You okay?" Gray asked as he brushed a gentle kiss over Luke's lips.

Luke managed a nod and dropped his arm. "It's almost too much, you know?"

Gray nodded in understanding. "You'll feel it soon."

"What?" Luke asked.

But Gray just smiled and then reached into his nightstand to pull out a bottle of lube. "I haven't been with anyone else," Gray suddenly said. "I can wear a condom until I get tested again to prove it. I don't even know about STDs with my condition ..."

Luke's passion cooled at Gray's telling statement and he wrapped his arms around Gray and rolled him to his back and pinned him with his gaze. "You never, *never* have to prove something like that to me because your word is good enough, do you hear me?" Luke said firmly. At Gray's slight nod, Luke whispered, "Someday I'm going to make you believe – really believe – that I didn't mean those shitty things I said." Luke kissed Gray long and hard until they were both squirming with renewed desire and then Luke rolled them over so he was on his back once more.

～

*G*ray's hands were shaking as he scooped up the discarded bottle of lube that had fallen onto the bed during their exchange. He hadn't realized until that moment how hung up he still was on the things Luke had said to him at the police station. Even as he'd followed Luke down the stairs to stop him from leaving, there'd been a tiny voice inside of him telling him what a fool he was – that one day Luke would shred him again with his words. But now that he could see the truth in Luke's eyes, could feel it in his touch, he knew he could put that day in the past where it belonged. He had a whole life of memories ahead of him with this man and he wouldn't tarnish any of them with the darkness that was born of one bad choice.

Gray remained where he was on top of Luke's warm, hard body as he slid his hand down to search out Luke's hole. He relished being able to see the reaction in Luke's eyes when Gray's finger played with him and then finally pushed inside of him. There was a little bit of everything there – fear, discomfort, awe, excitement, pleasure. But it was when Luke's eyes connected with his that he truly felt whatever it was that had linked them together from the moment they met.

"So good," Luke whispered as Gray's finger massaged him. He found the bundle of nerves he was seeking and wasn't surprised when Luke gasped and then lifted his whole body up as pleasure lanced through him. He kept up the gentle probing as he added a second finger and was pleased when Luke didn't react other than to beg him for more. Luke's cock was leaking against his own so Gray didn't linger for too long and when he finally began joining his and Luke's bodies together, he leaned down to whisper "love you" against Luke's lips just before he pushed forward.

～

*L*uke had been expecting the pain of Gray's entry but it didn't last long and once he got past the strangeness of feeling stuffed full, he managed to relax. The move allowed Gray to slip even farther inside of him and he groaned at the sensation of Gray's thighs brushing up against his ass. Gray had slipped his arms beneath Luke's legs to open him up as wide as possible and while he'd felt vulnerable at first, he quickly fell in love with the position because it allowed Gray to be as close to him as physically possible.

As Gray began sliding in and out of him in slow, leisurely strokes, a strange, burning sensation began in his ass and a twinge of worry went through him that the funky feeling would get worse. But instead, something else flared to life and the sensation disappeared altogether and was replaced with a tightening that began deep in his belly and continued to build as Gray moved in and out of him. The friction was intense because of Gray's size and Luke found himself incapable of speech as Gray's pace increased. He managed to return the soft kisses that Gray kept brushing over his lips but that didn't last long because Gray shifted the angle of his hips just a little bit and hot streaks of pleasure flashed through Luke's body. After that, Luke became a mass of grunts and moans and he could only follow as Gray took him higher and higher. And in that moment that he hung on the precipice and his eyes burned into Gray's, he felt it – what Gray had been talking about – that moment when no one and nothing else existed but the two of them and it was pure perfection.

And when he finally fell, Gray was there to catch him.

EPILOGUE

"*W*hat the fuck, Gray?!"

Gray smiled at the outraged shout and he looked down to see Ripley cocking her head curiously as heavy footsteps stomped towards them from the bedroom. He hit the send button on the email he'd just finished typing to his new agent and then closed the program.

"A cliff, Gray? He goes over a fucking cliff?" Luke shouted in disbelief as he held up the hardback as if to show Gray what he was referring to. Since Gray had been hearing the same reaction from a lot of his fans in the two weeks since his most recent *Nick Archer* book had been released, he just sat there and tried to bite back his smile. Luke's investment in the series had started once he managed to finish the first book shortly after they'd gotten settled in the cabin. Since then, he'd been maniacal about getting through all six books without receiving any spoilers from reviews or from Gray himself. And Gray had had a hell of a lot of fun hearing Luke wonder aloud about what would happen next to the harried Detective Archer.

"It's a fake out, right?" Luke asked. "He got out of the trunk before the car went over."

Gray just shrugged and Luke let out a colorful curse.

"Tell me," Luke finally ordered.

"Make me," Gray responded. Heat flared in Luke's eyes and by the time he'd dragged Gray out of his desk chair and kissed him into a stupor, he didn't seem to care anymore about what the plans for the next book were, if any. It was Gray who came to his senses before Luke could get his shirt completely unbuttoned.

"You'll be late for class," he murmured against Luke's lips.

"Shit," Luke muttered before placing another more chaste kiss on his mouth and drawing back. "Tonight," he warned.

"Dinner tonight at the ranch," Gray reminded him.

"Cancel," Luke quipped.

"Really?" Gray asked knowingly.

"No, not really," Luke bit out. "After," he said with a pointed glare and then he was leaning down to run his hand over Ripley's head. "Call your brother," he said for good measure before he leaned down and kissed Gray once more. "Love you," he said softly and a tremor went through Gray at the naked need he saw in the other man's eyes.

"Love you," Gray responded and it took everything in him to open the fist he had clenched in Luke's shirt.

Luke gave him one more longing look and then quickly left the cabin. Gray wasn't surprised when his phone beeped to indicate he had a new text. He chuckled when he saw the screen.

Tell me.

Another text appeared a second later.

No, don't.

Living together had been an easy decision after Luke left the military even after they'd asked him to come back after the truth about Shaw had been revealed. In truth, Gray would have gone anywhere Luke wanted and as much as he would have hated it, he would have supported any and all of Luke's future deployments. But the morning after he'd made love to Luke in L.A., Luke had told him he wanted to take classes so he could become a paramedic. Even though the decision to return to Dare had been Gray's, Luke hadn't hesitated for even a second since it meant he'd have the opportunity to rebuild his relationship with Rhys. They'd both had the chance to meet Rhys' lovers,

Callan and Finn, and he and Luke had been welcomed into the tight-knit, make-shift family that also included Dane, Jax and little Emma.

Gray's health had continued to improve and a subsequent visit to the doctor had shown no additional tumors. While the threat of reoccurrence would always be there, Gray knew he'd be able to get through it and not just because he had Luke by his side…no, he'd beat it because he had too much to live for now and not even cancer was going to take that from him.

The only sticking point for Gray had been Roman whom he hadn't seen or spoken to since his visit to the cabin shortly before Gray's chemo had ended. He'd been hopeful that Roman's message to him via Luke was a sign that they could build a relationship but every time Gray asked him to stop by Dare as he was passing through or to even call him, Roman sent a brief text to cancel. But Gray hadn't given up and it was with that thought in mind that he dialed the phone. There was no answer of course so he left his standard message before hanging up. A moment after he did, his phone rang but it wasn't Roman calling him.

"Hey," Gray said softly as he stood up and went to the couch to get more comfortable since he knew exactly why Luke was calling him. It was rare for Luke to make the entire drive to Missoula for his class without calling Gray just to check in and no matter what Gray was doing or where he was, he always had the same answer when Luke asked his catch-all question.

"Keep me company?" Luke asked.

"Always," Gray whispered.

The End

Scroll to the next page for a Sneak Peek of Roman's story

SNEAK PEEK

FINDING FORGIVENESS (FINDING SERIES, BOOK 4) (M/M)

TRIGGER WARNING

Note that this sneak peek contains a rape/dubious consent scene (not between the MCs)

PROLOGUE

"What can I get you?"

Roman Blackwell took one look at the bartender's cowboy hat and plaid shirt and guessed he wasn't going to find his favorite brand of whiskey in a place like this so he simply said "Scotch, neat" and then turned around to study the surprisingly busy club. He'd been to more gay clubs than he could count but this one was on the top of his "What were they thinking" list. There was the obligatory mirror ball above the dance floor but for the life of him, Roman couldn't figure out how it jived with the honky-tonk country music blaring from the antiquated sound system or the dark, wood paneled walls that looked like something you'd find in the house of a 70's sitcom family.

He'd had high hopes when the app on his phone had showed that a club called *Reds* was within a few miles of his hotel in the not so busy downtown section of Missoula, Montana but when he'd arrived, he'd found that the app had left out a strategic apostrophe and *Reds* was actually *Red's*. The sight of a few Harley Davidsons sitting out front among the half dozen pick-up trucks – two of which were attached to horse trailers – had been the deciding factor in whether he stayed or not. He'd always found bikers to be an interesting bunch when it came

157

to random hook-ups because despite their testosterone driven demeanors, tattoos and leather wear, they usually ended up being the guys that begged him the loudest to get them off when he had them pinned beneath him.

But despite the Harleys out front, he wasn't seeing any men who looked like they belonged to the Hogs. What he did see was a lot of cowboy hats, bolero neck ties, blue jeans and cowboy boots in all sorts of textures and colors. And the dancing...there wasn't a pole or cage in sight and while there were a few guys who might as well have been fucking on the dance floor considering all the gyrating they were doing, Roman was waiting for the moment when the whole group broke out into a line dance.

"Hey."

Roman glanced to his right and saw a pretty little thing sizing him up. No way the emo guy had been there a minute ago because he certainly would have noticed the full, pouty lips, nose piercing and hint of eyeliner framing bright blue eyes. A shot of lust went through Roman and he shifted his weight so he could give the guy his full attention.

"Buy me a drink?" the guy asked as he let his long fingers rub over his hip and down his thigh.

The bartender slid Roman's drink in front of him but instead of ordering the guy a drink, he took a swig of his own. Emo guy pouted prettily but didn't seem too disappointed because he sidled up even closer to Roman. But when he placed his hand on Roman's thigh and let it travel towards Roman's dick, Roman grabbed his wrist.

"Where is he?" Roman asked coolly as he took in the leather pants and vest the guy was wearing. There was no doubt the guy was linked to the still absent bikers but he definitely wasn't one himself.

"Who?"

Roman turned the guy's arm over and pointed to the tattoo on the guy's forearm. "Cooter," Roman said with a chuckle as he read the name tattooed beneath the words *Property of*.

"He's playing," Emo Guy said though from the smile on his face, whatever or whoever Cooter was playing with didn't seem to bother him. "Want to go watch?"

While Roman liked fucking bikers, he wasn't really interested in brawling with them over some boy toy that had so far only managed to get him half hard. But curiosity got the best of him so he gave the guy a brief nod and then swallowed the rest of his drink. Emo Guy took his hand and began leading him through the still sedate crowd of cowboys. Several of them openly stared at him and a few even sent him inviting looks but he ignored them. As they drew closer to the far side of the bar where a red curtain separated the main room from what he assumed was a private area, Roman could hear hearty laughs and deep, rumbling voices.

As Emo Guy pushed the curtain aside, Roman realized it wasn't a private area – it was just a room with a couple of pool tables. But that wasn't what had his attention. No, it was the half-naked guy bent over one of the pool tables that caught his eye along with the huge guy pounding into him from behind. Several other guys were standing around the table and a couple even had their cocks out and were stroking them as they urged the guy doing the fucking on.

The first thing Roman noticed about the guy getting fucked was how still he was as the biker rammed into him. His hands and cheek were pressed flat against the green felt. His shirt was still on but was pushed up to reveal a slim back and even under the dim light hanging above the table, Roman could see his hair was a startlingly shade of light blonde. His body kept jerking as he was brutally fucked but he made absolutely no sound and didn't struggle against the man holding his hips as he thrust into him. His eyes were open and staring in Roman's direction but not looking directly at him.

"Fuck, yeah!" one of the onlookers shouted as the guy doing the fucking cursed as he came. He held himself inside the guy for only a few seconds before pulling out and then another guy was stepping up and slamming into him.

"That's Cooter," Emo Guy said with pride.

Roman shook his head at the sickening sight. As much as it bothered him, especially considering how young the guy pinned to the table looked, he wasn't complaining about the harsh treatment and he didn't look drugged or drunk so Roman turned to leave. But just as he reached behind him to pull the curtain back, his eyes once again caught on the guy's and some unnamed emotion went through him when he saw how empty his gaze was – like he wasn't even there. He'd seen that look before and it had fucking haunted him his whole life.

"Such a pretty little slut," Cooter snarled as he fucked into the guy. His big hands reached up and fisted in the guy's hair and he yanked his head up and held it at an unnatural angle as he continued to brutalize him. The guy still didn't make a sound and when Cooter slammed his head back down on the table and pinned it there with his beefy hand, the guy's eyes looked exactly the same. Cooter grunted as he came and Roman felt the bile rise in his throat as he watched the man pull out and a trickle of blood ran down the guy's inner thigh.

"Bleeding just like a bitch," Cooter said in satisfaction and as the next guy moved into position, Roman dropped the curtain and began moving towards the pool table.

One of the bikers stepped in his path and said, "you gotta fucking wait your turn, man!"

But Roman just kneed him in the groin and then slammed his hand into his nose. The guy shouted in pain as he hit the ground and then Cooter was coming at him. Adrenaline surged through his blood as he saw a smattering of blood on the guy's condom covered cock and he didn't hesitate to slam his fist into Cooter's bulging neck. Cooter gasped and Roman hoped to God he'd managed to cause permanent damage to the man's trachea. The guy that was about to fuck the man on the table stepped back but Roman grabbed him by the balls and squeezed hard. The man screamed like a stuck pig and froze in place. The only two men still standing had enough sense to back off and one of them quickly tucked his own dick back in his pants as if to protect it from Roman's wrath.

"I suggest you take your friend there" – Roman motioned to Cooter who was struggling to draw in air – "and go before I rip your fucking balls from your body and jam them down his throat."

The biker he was holding on to nodded and as soon as Roman

released him, he and another guy dragged Cooter to his feet and helped him stumble out an emergency exit. Roman had no idea if Emo Guy had taken off when the whole thing started and he didn't care. All he cared about was that all the bikers were gone but he wasn't stupid enough to assume they wouldn't return once they had the chance to regroup. He turned to the pool table and saw that the guy hadn't even moved during the commotion but awareness had returned to his gaze and even though he lifted his head slightly to look over his shoulder at Roman, he didn't move otherwise. When he dropped his head back into the same exact position, a surge of anger went through Roman as he realized the man fully expected him to take the bikers' place. But his rage dissipated as he eyed the blood on the man's thigh.

Roman sucked in a couple of deep breaths and then reached down to pull the man's jeans up. He closed his hands over the man's upper arm and pulled him upright. Shock went through him as he got his first good look at the man's face and he realized that he wasn't a man...he was a fucking kid. Late teens maybe – twenty at the most.

"Do you need medical attention?" Roman asked as the kid finally reached down to zip up the pants that Roman was still holding up around his slim waist. As soon as he was done he shook Roman's hand off.

"You shouldn't have done that," was all the kid said as he ran a hand through his light hair. Roman didn't miss how striking the young man was but his affect was so fucked up that Roman didn't know what the hell he should do. Maybe if the kid had begged him to take him home or to the ER or even if he'd shown some sign of being intoxicated or drugged, Roman would have had a place to start but the guy was so disconnected from what had just happened that Roman was clueless. He had a very strong suspicion that if he just left him, he'd fold himself back over the pool table for the next guy who walked into the room. That or he'd go looking for the bikers so they could finish him off.

"Is there someone I can call for you?"

The kid shook his head and then pushed past Roman. But when he swayed and nearly fell, Roman grabbed him by the arm and made a decision that he knew he was going to regret come morning. "What's your name?"

"Hunter," came the disinterested response.

"You have two choices, Hunter. Either you tell me who to call to come get you or you're walking out of here with me right now."

Hunter's mossy green eyes looked around the room as if he was finally seeing it and then his gaze went to the pool table. "You," he finally said but he didn't take his eyes off the pool table until Roman pulled him from the room.

ABOUT THE AUTHOR

Dear Reader,

I hope you enjoyed Gray and Luke's story. They will be back in Roman and Hunter's story, Finding Forgiveness (Book 4, Finding Series) (M/M).

As an independent author, I am always grateful for feedback so if you have the time and desire, please leave a review, good or bad, so I can continue to find out what my readers like and don't like. You can also send me feedback via email at sloane@sloanekennedy.com

Join my Facebook Fan Group: Sloane's Secret Sinners

Connect with me:
www.sloanekennedy.com
sloane@sloanekennedy.com

ALSO BY SLOANE KENNEDY

(Note: Not all titles will be available on all retail sites)

The Escort Series
Gabriel's Rule (M/F)

Shane's Fall (M/F)

Logan's Need (M/M)

Barretti Security Series
Loving Vin (M/F)

Redeeming Rafe (M/M)

Saving Ren (M/M/M)

Freeing Zane (M/M)

Finding Series
Finding Home (M/M/M)

Finding Trust (M/M)

Finding Peace (M/M)

Finding Forgiveness (M/M)

Finding Hope (M/M/M)

The Protectors
Absolution (M/M/M)

Salvation (M/M)

Retribution (M/M)

Forsaken (M/M)

Vengeance (M/M/M)

A Protectors Family Christmas

Atonement (M/M)

Revelation (M/M)

Redemption (M/M)

Non-Series

Letting Go (M/F)

47632713R00105

Printed in Poland
by Amazon Fulfillment
Poland Sp. z o.o., Wrocław